THE LEGAL LIMIT

A HAL AND KRISTINA NOLAN LEGAL THRILLER

LARRY A. WINTERS

E-book ISBN: 979-8-9914997-1-2

Paperback ISBN: 979-8-9914997-2-9

Hardcover ISBN: 979-8-9914997-3-6

1

———————

HAL NOLAN COULDN'T HELP but smirk as he watched the news reports blaze across the wall-mounted TV. Garrison Whitehead, hedge fund mogul and accused fraudster, exonerated on all charges.

Hal clinked his champagne flute against Kristina's. "You know what? Winning is really fun."

Kristina arched an eyebrow. "Your insightfulness never ceases to amaze me."

"I'm serious. As much as I enjoy the fight—and you know I do—there's nothing better than basking in the sweet, sweet moment of victory."

The TV drew his attention again, a perfectly-coiffed news anchor saying, "This has got to be a major blow for the Philadelphia District Attorney's Office, which had dubbed Whitehead's trial 'the fraud case of the decade.' And it marks yet another high-profile victory for The Nolan Law Firm, a rising legal powerhouse...."

"Powerhouse!" Hal's smirk bloomed into a full-fledged smile. If there was a better high than being praised by a stranger whose opinion meant nothing, he had yet to discover it.

Kristina watched him with an all-too-familiar look of bemusement and exasperation.

"What?" he said. "Can't a man enjoy the fruits of his labor?"

"*Our* labor," she said. "And yes, enjoy it. Just don't let it go to your head." She smiled and tiny dimples appeared at the corners of her mouth.

Hal glided his conference room chair closer to hers, wrapped an arm around her shoulders, and pulled their chairs together with a thud. He nuzzled his face against hers—one of the perks of being married to your law partner—and managed to get a little laugh out of her.

"Come on, Kristina." He pushed her hair behind her ear and kissed the corner of her eye, her cheek, her throat. "This is it— what we've been working toward all these years. Are you really going to pretend you're not bursting with happiness right now?"

She leaned into him, those dimples appearing again. "It does feel nice to be doing well," she conceded.

"*Doing well?* We're crushing it! Look at this conference room!" He swept his arm to indicate the sleek gleaming table, the supple leather chairs, the floor-to-ceiling windows with their panoramic view of the Philly skyline.

Kristina shook her head, but he saw the pride in her eyes. It was a look he'd fallen in love with years ago, back when they were young law students dreaming of starting their own firm. Now, here they were. *A powerhouse.*

"We finally have cash in the bank. Finally have clients at the door. Hell, we have *employees*—actual lawyers, working for *us*! We're drinking a thousand-dollar bottle of champagne. And the best part is, we're only getting started. With the Whitehead win, we're about to become the most sought-after criminal defense firm in the city."

She took his hand, squeezed it. "I know. I'm excited, too."

The door burst open, cutting off their conversation. Their

office manager stood in the doorway. Her face was pale. "I'm sorry to interrupt," she said, her voice quavering. "I know you're celebrating, but ... something's wrong with the computer system."

Hal felt his smile falter. Priscilla was usually imperturbable. He exchanged a glance with Kristina.

"What do you mean, *wrong*?" Kristina said.

"I don't know exactly." Priscilla's hands twisted in front of her. "Everything's ... locked up. No one can access any files, and there's this message on all the screens."

"What message?" Hal said.

Priscilla winced. "Maybe you better look at it yourself."

Hal rose from his chair and set his champagne flute on the table beside the sweating bottle. Kristina was already following Priscilla out the door to the main office.

A scene of chaos greeted them there. Associates and paralegals clustered around computers, arguing urgently with each other, their expressions filled with confusion and dread. They fell silent as Hal stepped into their midst.

Every screen's display was identical—a stylized skull and crossbones. A timer counting down. And beneath the timer, in all-caps, four words.

GO TO HELL HAL.

"Well that's hurtful."

Kristina's face paled. "It's a ransomware attack."

2

Hours later, FBI agents and cybersecurity consultants filled their office. Despite their frenzied work, the message continued to pulse from every screen.

GO TO HELL HAL.

The relentless countdown was now accompanied by a ransom demand so astronomical that just looking at it sent jolts of nausea through Hal.

"Why do they assume we know how to get bitcoin? Who the hell knows how to get bitcoin?"

"I've got someone working on it," Kristina said. Her voice was barely audible over the tumult around them. "Just in case."

He gawked at her. "You're considering paying the ransom?"

"Keeping our options open."

Dread gnawed at his insides as he watched the grim-faced FBI agents work. With the possible exception of Kristina, he'd always prided himself on being the smartest person in the room —especially *this room*—but the cyberattack had reduced him to a helpless spectator.

One of the cybersecurity experts gestured to Kristina. She nodded to him. "I'll be right back."

As Kristina threaded her way through the chaos, one of the agents approached Hal. Hal braced himself. The FBI's "Special Agent in Charge" Charles Cooley—a tall man whose plain gray suit and 1950s haircut marked him as the type of self-important government drone Hal loved eviscerating in court. Having to depend on him now was a new experience, and not a pleasant one.

"Mr. Nolan."

"Just call me Hal, okay?"

"We're working hard, but...." Cooley's voice trailed off.

"But you're not going to crack this one before that timer hits zero, are you?"

Cooley cleared his throat. "Unless you can think of someone with a motive to target you? Someone with a personal vendetta?" He gestured at one of the screens. "For a ransomware attack, the message is unusually personal."

GO TO HELL HAL.

Hal let out a harsh laugh, rubbing his temples. He was a criminal defense attorney. Between the victims whose tormentors he'd set free, and the monsters whose trials he'd lost, and the cops whose careers he'd napalmed, there were literally hundreds of people who despised him. "No one specific comes to mind because the list is too damn long."

"Well, give it some thought. If anyone comes to mind, let me know."

"Sure."

Hal's gaze drifted to one of the screens, the ominous countdown and the sky-high ransom demand. Then he looked at Kristina, still talking to the cybersecurity consultant at the far side of the room. Cooley followed his gaze.

"I need to remind you, Mr. Nolan, that the FBI strongly discourages paying ransoms in cases like this. It only encourages—"

"More attacks." Hal cut him off. "But ultimately, it's our decision to make, right?"

"That's correct," Cooley conceded, his expression softening slightly. Given Cooley's tenure at the FBI, he had to have tangled with his share of defense attorneys, but if he took any pleasure in Hal's misery, he wasn't showing it. "I'm sorry we can't be of more help, Mr. Nolan."

Hal sighed. "I appreciate all you're doing."

Hal caught Kristina's eye as she made her way back to him. "We need to talk in private." She inclined her head toward his office.

Hal followed her, closing the door behind them. The sudden quiet was jarring after the noise outside. For a moment, they just stood there breathing.

"What did Cooley say?" Kristina asked.

"Not much." He moved behind his giant desk, one of the first things they'd bought when The Nolan Law Firm had begun to enjoy some success. "The FBI hasn't identified the hacker. I guess we have a choice to make. Pay or call their bluff."

"Call their bluff?" Kristina's eyes narrowed. "You talk about this like it's a game."

"Do I look like I'm having fun?"

She leaned against the wall, looked away. "No."

"You saw the number they're demanding. If we pay it, the firm will be broke." Hal ran a hand through his hair.

"They have access to our network, Hal. To our data. If we don't pay the demand, we risk them releasing our clients' secrets across the Internet. Can you imagine the reputational harm? Not to mention our clients will sue us into oblivion."

Hal scoffed. "It would take years for those lawsuits to crawl through the court system. And we know how to create delays."

"Are you serious right now, Hal?" Kristina came toward his desk, looking exasperated. "We have an ethical obligation to our clients, and you're talking about outmaneuvering them in court?"

"You know I didn't mean it that way."

"Do you want to be known as the law firm that betrayed its clients to save its own skin? Loyalty matters."

"Loyalty?" Hal shook his head. "How loyal do you think our big-shot clients will be once they see us operating out of a cardboard box? They'll repay our selfless sacrifice by dumping our asses."

"We have to make a choice, Hal. And the clock is ticking."

Hal glanced at the countdown timer on his monitor, less than an hour remaining. They'd built this firm from nothing, clawed their way to the top through sheer determination. The thought of losing it all made him physically ill. But Kristina was right—they had a choice to make and they had to get it right.

He rose from his desk and crossed to the window, looking out at the Philadelphia skyline. "Alright, let's think through the pros and cons. Option One—we pay the bastards."

Kristina nodded. "Pro—we protect our clients."

"Con—we're broke," Hal said. "Worse than broke. In a hole we'll never climb out of."

A heavy silence filled the office, broken only by the muffled sounds of the FBI agents working outside. Kristina joined him at the window.

"Option Two," she said, meeting his gaze, "we don't pay."

"Pro—we keep our money," Hal said. "We save the firm."

"Con," Kristina put in, "if they're not bluffing, our clients' info gets leaked and our reputation for protecting our clients is destroyed."

"Pro—we don't fund criminals."

"Hold on," Kristina said. "You already did your Pro for Option Two. You can't add more Pros."

"There's no rule against adding more Pros."

"Then I can add more Pros to Option One," she said.

"Go for it."

Kristina straightened. "Option One. Pay the ransom and protect our clients who trusted us with their secrets. Pro—we do what we're meant to do. We serve our clients, instead of ourselves. We act like *lawyers*."

They stood in silence for a moment, staring at each other. "Kristina...."

"The bitcoin transaction is ready to go," she said. "I know the financial loss will hurt—"

"It will *devastate* the firm."

"But we'll know we did everything we could to protect the people who trusted us."

Hal pulled in a deep and ragged breath. Protect the firm, or protect the clients? He looked at his gleaming office, the embodiment of his dreams. He looked at Kristina, the woman who'd built all of this at his side. He looked at the words. *GO TO HELL HAL.*

"This needs to be a joint decision," Kristina said. "I won't do it unless you agree."

3

———

HAL'S EYES burned as he squinted at a computer screen, the harsh glow competing with the sunlight streaming through the grimy windows. He re-read a discovery motion that had taken him forty minutes to write. Even if he rounded up, and billed the client for one hour, it wouldn't be enough to pay even one of the bills stacked on the corner of his desk. Could he stretch it to one-point-two hours?

He laughed despite himself. The irony of over-billing a client who was charged with petty theft was not lost on him. *Petty theft.* A far cry from the high-profile work he'd become used to, but beggars couldn't be choosers.

And right now, he and Kristina were definitely beggars.

Four months had passed and he still marveled at how quickly it had all fallen apart. One moment, they were basking in the triumph of winning the fraud case of the decade—a rising legal powerhouse. And the next....

We made the noble choice.

Hal surveyed the two-hundred square feet of squalor that had become the new home of The Nolan Law Firm. Fading paint, water-stained ceiling, two mismatched desks crammed against opposite walls and a battered conference table in between. The view from their ground-floor windows showcased one of Philadelphia's least desirable neighborhoods.

He'd joked to Kristina that setting up shop in a high-crime area was like free advertising, and they could count on an endless stream of walk-in clients. But the clients hadn't walked in, and the only thing they could count on was the constant threat of eviction.

Hal leaned back in his chair, wincing as it tilted dangerously. Everything in this hole was on the verge of collapse.

His gaze slid to the stack of bills. *Just like the old days*. He and Kristina had clawed their way up from the bottom once before. Now, they were right back where they started. *GO TO HELL HAL*.

Hell indeed. Whoever wrote those words sure got their wish.

Kristina was in court, defending some poor schmuck charged with public urination. The thought of his wife, with her brilliant legal mind, reduced to taking any client off the street, sent a pang of agony through his chest. She deserved so much better.

He returned his attention to the document on his screen, determined to stretch the task into at least one billable hour, when a knock at the door jolted him from his thoughts.

He froze, heart racing, not sure he'd really heard anything. At the sound of a second knock, he launched from his chair. He hurriedly straightened his rumpled shirt and tie and shoved his arms into a sport jacket.

He opened the door, praying to find a new client on the other side and not a bill collector. "Welcome to The Nolan Law Firm—" The words died in his throat as he found himself face to face with a ghost from his past.

Ariana Hess stood in the doorway, looking as stunning as she had in high school. Time had been kind to her, refining her beauty rather than diminishing it. Her long red hair cascaded over her shoulders, framing a face that had haunted Hal's adolescent dreams—not all of them dry—more times than he cared to admit. Those piercing green eyes locked onto his, and for a moment, Hal forgot how to breathe.

"Hal Nolan," she said. "Been a while."

Hal swallowed. "Ariana," he managed, acutely aware of his disheveled appearance and the shabby office behind him. His palms were suddenly slick, his mouth dry.

A smirk played on her lips, and he could swear she actually looked him up and down. "Are you going to invite me in?"

Hal winced. "Of course. Yeah." As she brushed past him, their arms touched and she gave him that smirk again. She hadn't changed, still the ultra-confident girl from high school, the head cheerleader, the prom queen. His first girlfriend.

"Nice place," Ariana said, her tone making it clear she thought it was anything but. She turned to face him, twirling a strand of her hair around one perfectly manicured finger. "I thought you became some fancy lawyer."

Hal tried not to bristle at the comment. "I did. This is ... a temporary cash flow issue. Nothing we can't handle."

She nodded, but didn't look convinced. "It wasn't easy finding your firm's address."

"Our ad budget is constrained at the moment. What brings you here? It's been what, ten years since high school?"

"Fourteen."

"Well, you should have visited four months ago. You would have been much more impressed."

"I didn't need you four months ago. Now, I...." She seemed unable to continue.

Hal studied her face, noticing for the first time the strain around her eyes, the slight tremor in her hand when she continued to tug at her hair. "What's going on, Ariana?" Despite everything, seeing her in distress stirred something in him. Old feelings, long buried, threatened to surface.

Ariana drew an unsteady breath. "My sister is in trouble —*real trouble.*"

"Paige?" Hal tried to imagine what kind of trouble Ariana's straight-laced younger sister could possibly be in.

"I know, right." Ariana let out an awkward laugh. "Goody-two-shoes Paige, who reported herself for accidentally keeping a library book too long." She met his gaze, suddenly serious again. "Hal, I don't know what's going on here." She gestured at the secondhand furniture and yellowing walls. "But I know you. I know you can help her."

Hal's mind raced. Part of him wanted to laugh—here he was, barely keeping his head above water, and she thought he was the answer to her problems? But another part, the part of him that had never quite gotten over Ariana Hess, leaned in.

"Exactly what kind of trouble are we talking about?"

4

———

Kristina Nolan pondered public urination as she approached the door to their office. She had assumed she would plead the case out—it was only a misdemeanor—but her client turned out to be surprisingly adamant about not taking any deals. That meant she'd have to build an actual defense. No easy task, given the witness statements and security camera footage showing him spraying the plate-glass windows of *Celene Jewelers* like he was trying to power-wash them.

Public urination. She smiled and shook her head. It might be far from the heady heights of the Whitehead fraud trial, but it was still a trial. Still work.

As she reached for the door, she heard muffled voices inside. Hal wasn't alone, and the other voice sounded like a woman's. Curiosity piqued, Kristina pushed the door open.

She froze in the doorway. Hal stood uncomfortably close to a striking redhead, whose hand rested on his arm. The woman's eyes flicked toward Kristina, and Kristina was sure she saw a flash of annoyance, even though the woman masked it quickly.

"Kristina." Hal took a quick step back from the redhead.

"You're back early." His voice held a guilty note that Kristina didn't like. At all.

"Did I walk in on something?"

"Just a client meeting. I thought you had a meeting with the DA?"

Kristina's gaze swept from Hal to the unknown woman and back again. "It ended early. The urinator refused to settle."

Hal cleared his throat. "Well, this is ... good timing. I'm glad you're here. Kristina, this is Ariana Hess. An old friend. Ariana, my wife and law partner, Kristina."

Ariana extended a hand. "Nice to meet you." Her smile didn't even come close to reaching her eyes.

Kristina shook the offered hand and responded with an equally insincere smile. "Hal's never mentioned you before."

"Oh, we go way back. High school sweethearts."

Kristina let her eyebrows rise as she turned to Hal, who looked like he'd rather be anywhere else right now. "Wow. High school sweethearts?"

"Ariana was the head cheerleader. I was the class clown. It didn't last long." Hal's face was bright red, which she would have found endearing under just about any other circumstances. Visibly pulling himself together, he gestured to the chairs in front of their battered conference table. "Why don't we all sit down? Ariana was just about to explain why she's here."

As they settled into their seats, Kristina watched Ariana closely. The woman exuded confidence and a kind of brash sexuality, but there was an undercurrent of tension in the set of her shoulders, a tightness around her eyes, that softened Kristina's initial impression—but only slightly.

"Go ahead, Ariana," Hal said, leaning forward in his chair. "You were saying your sister is in trouble?"

"She's been arrested," Ariana said, her voice catching. "For vehicular homicide. They're saying she … she hit someone—a cop—and left him to die on the road."

There was genuine distress in the woman's voice. Kristina said, "Why don't you slow down. Tell us what happened. Start at the beginning."

Ariana took a deep breath. "All I know is the police went to her apartment a few nights ago. They arrested her, saying she killed this cop. She's been in jail since."

Kristina glanced at Hal, who looked almost as distressed as Ariana. "Homicide by vehicle is a serious charge," she said. "What evidence do the police have that your sister did this?"

"I … I don't know. But there's no way Paige would do that. Not Paige. Hal, you knew her. Even if … even if she had an accident and hit someone, you know she wouldn't leave them there."

"Do you know if she was drinking?" Hal said. "Was she over the legal limit when this alleged incident happened?"

"I don't know. She's not a big drinker. She could never do something like this. She's a teacher."

"Paige wants us to represent her?" Hal said.

"Well," Ariana looked away. "I haven't talked to her about it. But she needs a lawyer. And you—" Her voice cut off as she glanced at Kristina.

"What were you going to say?" Kristina said.

Ariana hesitated. "I know Hal. I know how smart he is, how persuasive. If anyone can save Paige, it's him."

Kristina could feel Hal's nervous gaze on her, gauging her reaction to his ex-girlfriend's praise. She managed to keep her face neutral.

"Hal and I will need to discuss this. As I'm sure you understand, we're very selective about the cases we take on."

"Of course." Regaining some of her earlier composure, Ariana rose gracefully from her chair. "I know your schedule must be hectic. But please, if there's any way you can take this on.... Paige is a good person and she needs help."

Kristina watched as Hal escorted Ariana to the door. Before stepping outside, Ariana placed a hand on his shoulder. "Thank you for hearing me out, Hal. It's ... it's good to see you." As the door closed behind her, Kristina let out a breath.

Hal turned to face her. "I know what you're thinking, Kristina."

Kristina arched an eyebrow. "About your high school sweetheart or her sister's case?"

At least Hal had the grace to look abashed. "We dated for a month or two, and it was a lifetime ago. Ancient history."

"It doesn't seem like ancient history to Ariana. She couldn't keep her hands off you."

"That's just how she is. It doesn't mean anything."

"She was flirting with you."

He laughed uneasily. "She wasn't."

"She was. Right in front of me. Do you not understand how disrespectful that is?"

"Okay, yes, I do, and I'm sorry you had to experience that. But Kristina ... we're talking about a murder trial!"

"Homicide by vehicle, not murder."

"The next best thing!" The way Hal's eyes lit up both exasperated and charmed her. "You have to admit it's a hell of an upgrade from petty theft and public urination. And the victim was a cop? That could make headlines."

Kristina pinched the bridge of her nose. She hated that her emotions were so conflicted—affected by jealousy of all things! But Hal was *her* class clown, and she couldn't get over how Ariana had looked at him.

"Do we even know if Paige can afford to pay us?" she said. "A trial like this could go on for months, especially if the DA's Office digs in—and they probably will, if the victim was a cop. Ariana said Paige is a teacher...."

Hal waved a hand. "We can work for free if we have to. Think about the media coverage, the publicity if we win. We'll start getting real clients again. We'll be able to move out of this dump." He met her gaze. "This is our chance, Kristina. Please don't throw it away because of Ariana. Maybe you don't trust her, but you know you can trust me."

Kristina closed her eyes. Of course she could trust Hal. They'd been together since law school. He'd always been faithful. He loved her as much as she loved him—maybe more. He'd taken a bullet for her.

She might be able to talk him out of taking this case—she *probably* could—but would that be fair to him, to their firm?

She opened her eyes and met his gaze. "Let's find out what jail Paige is in, set up a visit, get her story."

"Visiting an accused murderer in jail." A grin spread across his face. "Just like old times."

Kristina managed a smile of her own, even as she fought down a surge of anxiety. "Just like old times."

5

———

THE PHILADELPHIA INDUSTRIAL CORRECTIONAL CENTER loomed before them, a sprawling complex of reddish-brown brick and concrete. High walls stretched in every direction, coils of razor wire gleamed in the hazy sunlight, and security cameras leaned down, watching.

Hal's smile bubbled out of him as he glanced at Kristina. "Feels good to be back, huh?"

Kristina crossed her arms over her chest. "Hal, this is a jail. People are suffering...."

"Come on, Kristina. Admit it."

He was rewarded with a hint of a smile. "Fine. It feels a little good to be back."

They made their way toward the main entrance. For Hal, the weathered *Philadelphia Industrial Correctional Center* sign might as well be a *Welcome Home* banner. As they approached the heavy doors, he took a deep breath, savoring the wonderful aroma.

Inside, Hal plastered on his most charming smile as they approached the security checkpoint. "Morning, gentlemen." He flourished his identification at two bored-looking security officers. "Hal and Kristina Nolan to see Paige Hess."

The officers barely looked up. One of them—a grizzled giant Hal recognized from prior visits—muttered under his breath. "Been a while, Nolan."

"Miss us?"

The officer took their IDs with deliberate slowness. "Thought you might have retired."

"Not a chance."

"Wait over there."

"But we scheduled a meeting for—"

"Wait over there," the officer repeated, an edge in his voice.

Hal's smile faltered as he and Kristina headed over to a row of uncomfortable plastic chairs against the wall. "They're making us wait on purpose, trying to throw us off our game."

"Or they're just busy, Hal. Not everything is personal."

He knew she was probably right, but everything had started to seem personal to him after the cyberattack. *GO TO HELL HAL.*

He forced away the thought and tried to focus his mind on business. "I hope no one beat us to her. A lot of lawyers will see the potential here."

"Hal," Kristina put her hand on his arm. "Relax."

Before Hal could respond, a different officer approached. He planted himself in front of them, thumbs hooked in his belt. "Well if it isn't the shadiest pair of shysters in Philadelphia. I thought I smelled bullshit in the air."

"Officer Velazquez." Hal couldn't help grinning. "Pretty sure you're smelling your own armpits. You know, they make deodorant for that. Also, we prefer the term *legal powerhouse.*"

"Uh-huh. How you doing, Kristina?"

"Doing well. How are Renata and the girls?"

"Everyone's doing great." Velazquez's gaze returned to Hal, his smile vanishing instantly. "Follow me, shysters."

As the officer led them through a series of heavy security doors, Hal's mood improved again, each buzz and clang increasing his giddiness. He leaned close to Kristina's ear as they walked. "Sure beats your public urination case, huh?"

"Please try to look appropriately grave when we meet the woman who's facing down a homicide accusation, okay?"

Hal fist-pumped the air. "Back in the game, baby!"

Velazquez shook his head and let them into a small, windowless room furnished with an ill-treated metal table and four chairs, all welded to the floor.

"Wait here," he said. "I'll be back with your client."

"Prospective client," Hal said.

Velazquez's face brightened. "Good—poor girl's still got a chance."

As the door slammed shut behind Velazquez, Hal turned to Kristina. "Don't you love the banter?"

"I'm not sure that was banter." Kristina's lips thinned. "So you knew this girl when you were in high school? Your cheerleader girlfriend's sister?"

He ignored the jibe about Ariana. "Paige Hess. Straight-A student. Never broke a rule in her life. You would have liked her."

"And yet you chose the sister. More your type?"

Hal made a face. "I only have one type, Kristina—"

The door opened again. Velazquez ushered in a young woman, her hands cuffed in front of her. Paige Hess looked just like Hal remembered her from high school. Plain, small, nothing like her sister. Where Ariana exuded confidence and hotness, Paige seemed to shrink into herself, as if trying to blend into the room. Hal wondered again how the hell she'd ended up in this mess.

Velazquez removed her handcuffs without a word, then left the room.

"Paige." Hal stepped forward, considered hugging her, then self-consciously patted her arm instead.

"Hello Hal."

He forced a smile. "It's good to see you again. I wish the circumstances were better."

They regarded each other for a moment, an awkward reunion. Hal cleared his throat. "This is my wife and law partner, Kristina."

"Ariana sent you?" Paige said.

"She asked us to represent you," Hal said. "Assuming you want us."

Paige hesitated before shaking their hands. "Thank you for coming," she said softly. "I ... I don't know what to do. They're saying I killed someone."

Hal nodded sympathetically. "We understand. But before we get into details, there's something we need to take care of first." He pulled out the retainer agreement, placing it on the table. "If you could just sign this, it'll ensure everything we discuss is protected by the attorney-client privilege."

Paige sat in one of the metal chairs. Hal and Kristina took two of the other seats. Paige skimmed the document, actually reading it. Hal supposed there was a first time for everything.

The teacher looked up at them. "This looks fine, but ... you don't want to hear my story first?"

Hal opened his mouth to respond, but Kristina cut in smoothly. "Of course we do. But Hal is right—it's better if we formalize our relationship first. That way, we can all speak freely."

Paige nodded slowly, taking the pen Hal offered. As she signed, Hal felt a weight lift from his shoulders. Their representation of an accused killer was official. They were back in the game.

"Alright, Paige," he said, leaning forward. "Tell us what happened."

Paige took a deep breath. "I was driving home from my book club and I was pulled over by a cop."

"Approximately what time was this?"

"I don't know. Close to midnight, I guess? He thought I was driving drunk."

"Were you?"

Paige shook her head. "I had a glass of wine at the book club, but I was fine. The cop asked me to get out of my car, did some sobriety tests, made me do a breathalyzer. The results must have shown I was sober, because he apologized for stopping me and let me go."

"Did he say why he thought you were drunk?" Kristina said.

"He mentioned my driving looked erratic." Paige shrugged. "Maybe I got distracted and crossed over the line for a second? I don't really remember."

"Did he say anything else?"

"He asked about my car—it's a Ford Explorer. The front was damaged and he wanted to know what happened. I told him the truth—that I had hit a deer a few days before and hadn't had a chance to take the car in yet. He told me I should have it looked at, make sure it's safe to drive." She paused. "He seemed like a nice guy."

"Did you get his name?" Kristina said.

"Sorry, no."

"That's okay," Hal said. "We'll get that information. So after he let you go, what next? It was late. I assume you drove straight home?"

Paige nodded. "And a little later—maybe thirty minutes?—there was a knock on my apartment door. It wasn't the same cop.

This one wore regular clothes. A leather jacket. He said he was a detective."

"Did he tell you his name? Again, if you don't have it, that's okay—"

"No, this name I remember." Her eyes seemed to darken. "Mateo Avalos."

Hal tried to keep the reaction from his face, but couldn't help exchanging a quick glance with Kristina. If Detective Avalos was involved, they had their work cut out for them.

"He said he had a warrant for my car," Paige said. "Told me they were towing it right then. I asked why, and he told me before he answered that he needed to explain my rights."

"Did he?" Kristina said.

"Yes. The right to remain silent, all that." Her voice hitched. "And he took me to the police station."

"*Did* you remain silent?" Hal said.

"No, I ... I wanted to know why I was there. I asked. And Detective Avalos said I'd hit a man with my car and left him in the street. He said it happened in front of some sports bar—Foul Line? He said the person I hit was a cop, and a lot of people were very angry, but that if I told him everything maybe he could help me."

Help her right into a prison cell.

"You should have asked for a lawyer," Kristina said.

Paige nodded. "I know. I wasn't thinking straight."

"Cops like Avalos, they're very good at twisting people's words. Anything you said to him can be used against you at trial."

Paige's eyes widened. "Is there going to be a trial?"

"Hold on," Hal said. "Let's not get ahead of ourselves. What did you tell Detective Avalos?"

"That it wasn't me. My drive home from the book club did take me past that bar, yes, but I never hit anyone."

"You admitted you drove past the bar?" Kristina said.

"Is that bad?"

"Did you tell him anything else?" Hal said. "Please try to remember. It could be important."

"I don't think so." Paige shook her head, but she looked less certain now. "I just told him he'd made a mistake, that it wasn't me."

"Did he tell you the name of the victim—the cop you supposedly hit?" Kristina said.

"I don't think so. If he did, I don't remember."

Hal's mind was already searching out potential angles, and a glance at Kristina told him she was doing the same. "Okay," he said. "Paige, we're going to find a way to fix this."

"Can you get me out of here?" Paige gestured at their surroundings, a note of panic in her voice.

"Our first step will be your bail hearing," Kristina said. Her voice was gentle, sympathetic, and Hal knew it wasn't an act. "We'll try to get you released on bail while we prepare your defense."

Paige shifted awkwardly in her metal chair. "Bail? Will that be ... a lot?"

Hal waved away her concern. "We'll push the magistrate judge to set a reasonable amount, and you won't even need to pay that. A bail bondsmen will post most of the money and all you'll need to put up is ten percent."

Paige nodded, seeming to take this in. "And your fees?"

"We can worry about that later." Hal caught Kristina's sharp look but ignored it. Money would be nice, but he still thought this case was worth taking on for free, for the publicity alone. They would figure out the finances—they always did.

Outside the prison, Hal turned to Kristina. "Mateo Avalos. I can't wait to cross-examine that jerk again."

"We've got a long way to go before we're cross-examining

anyone. And thanks to your generosity, we're going to be severely limited in our resources."

Hal's enthusiasm dimmed, but only slightly. "We'll need an investigator. What about that guy we used on the Weiss case?"

"Too expensive. I was thinking Lena."

Hal frowned. "Lena, as in your *cousin* Lena?"

"She's an investigator. A good one."

"Lena is.... Look, she's great, but we need someone who can think outside the box."

Kristina's jaw tightened. "You mean someone who's willing to bend the rules, like you. Lena's thorough and reliable. And she's family. I'm hoping she'll help us as a favor."

"Lena Randall doing a favor for *me?*" He laughed and shook his head. "Trust me, Kristina, we will never see that day. Or have you forgotten what happened at our rehearsal dinner?"

"I'll talk to her."

Hal knew that tone. There would be no arguing with Kristina on this point. He sighed. "Fine. Talk to her."

As they walked to their car—a battered Toyota Camry with rust spots and 200,000 miles on the odometer—Hal's mind was already scheming. This case could be their salvation. Or possibly the final slide into bankruptcy. Either way, there was no turning back now. The signed retainer letter was in his pocket.

For better or worse, they were committed.

6

————

Later that night, Kristina stepped into a 24-hour laundromat, a bell tinkling softly above her head. Harsh fluorescent lights reflected off rows of humming washers and dryers, and the air was thick with the scent of detergent and fabric softener. She spotted Lena Randall immediately, her short dark hair and ramrod-straight posture standing out among the slouching night owls folding their laundry. Lena was methodically transferring clothes from a washer to a dryer, her movements so precise and economical Kristina had to smile.

She walked up beside Lena, pretty sure the woman sensed her presence even if she chose not to look up from her task. "Hey, cuz. Your roommate told me I'd find you here."

"Bit late for a social call, Kristina."

"This isn't a social call." Kristina lowered her voice, thankful that the whir and thrum of the machines provided a measure of privacy. She leaned against an unused washer. "It's business."

Now Lena did look up, her eyes narrowing slightly as she closed the dryer door with a definitive click. She gestured to a pair of rickety chairs in the corner. As they sat down, Kristina couldn't help but notice the dark circles under Lena's eyes, her old clothes, her worn handbag. Apparently The Nolan Law Firm wasn't the only local business struggling to make ends meet. The realization brought a twinge of guilt for what she was about to ask.

"I have a case," Kristina began, leaning in close. "It could be big. High profile, high stakes. We need an investigator we can trust."

"And you thought of me?" Lena's eyes narrowed. "What's the catch?"

"What are you talking about, Lena?" Kristina forced a laugh, but it sounded so fake she winced.

"I'm talking about Hal swearing he'd never hire me again after the Grimes trial. So what's the catch?"

Kristina looked away. Across the room, a woman wrestled what looked like a sleeping bag into a washing machine, straining with the exertion.

"Kristina?" Lena prompted.

Kristina felt her shoulders sag. "The catch is we can't pay you. Not your usual rate, anyway."

"Because of that cyberattack?"

"It was a ransomware attack. We paid the demand, but it cost us everything. We had to let the staff go, negotiate an early termination of our lease ... and even then we could barely pay the demand. It's all gone, everything. We're rebuilding from scratch."

"Jesus," Lena muttered, her expression softening. "I didn't realize it was that bad."

"We tried to keep it quiet." Her fingers absently traced the pearl necklace at her throat, one of the few valuables she'd been unable to part with. "But we have a client now, a chance to get back on our feet. That's why I'm here, hoping you might consider taking it on as a personal favor."

Lena seemed to study her, her gaze penetrating. Even

though they were cousins, as kids they had often been mistaken for sisters. They shared the same almond-shaped eyes, the same high cheekbones, the same auburn hair. But their differences had manifested in adulthood. Lena was tall, sculpted, her body composed of lean muscle and a hard athleticism shaped by her service in the Marine Corps. Kristina was softer, smoother, the result of a life spent mostly inside books and her own head. Even so, holding Lena's gaze was uncannily like meeting her own eyes in a mirror.

"A favor," Lena said skeptically. "For you, or for Hal?"

Kristina felt a flicker of defensiveness. "For both of us. Hal and I are a team."

"A team where one member is an attention-starved sleaze," Lena said. "I'll never understand what you see in that man."

Kristina felt her back stiffen. "He almost died for me, for one thing. And he's not a sleaze. He's just not as ... straight-laced as some people—"

"As me, you mean." Lena shook her head. "I love you, Kristina. And I respect you. But Hal's tactics ... they're going to get you in trouble one day. Especially now that you're in this position."

Kristina fought to keep her expression neutral. "Hal pushes the boundaries, but he would never do anything to jeopardize our firm."

Lena's skepticism was palpable. "You sure about that? Because from where I'm sitting, it looks like you're both backed into a corner, and desperate people make desperate choices."

"We're not desperate," Kristina snapped, even as a small voice in her head whispered that they absolutely were. "We're determined. There's a difference."

Lena studied her for a long moment, the hum of the laundromat machines filling the silence between them. Finally, she spoke. "Alright. A favor then."

Kristina felt a surge of relief. "Let's take a walk. I'll give you the facts."

Outside, the air was pleasantly cool. As they walked the mostly empty streets of Center City, Kristina launched into Paige's story—the traffic stop, the police interrogation, the arrest. Lena listened intently, silently absorbing the details.

"What's your gut telling you?" Lena said.

"What do you mean?"

"You know what I mean. Did she run over the cop or not?"

"That doesn't matter. As her lawyer—"

Lena stopped walking. "Come on. It's just us girls."

Kristina hesitated, then laughed. "I'm not sure. She seems sincere, but ... her story about hitting a deer seems too convenient. And her sister—" She closed her mouth, but not before Lena caught her tone.

"What about her sister?"

"That's how we got the case. Paige's sister is Hal's ex-girlfriend from high school. And she's ... very attractive."

Lena's eyes widened. "No shit?"

"Don't give me that look," Kristina said. "What, are you *enjoying* this?"

Lena laughed. "Sorry—I don't get many opportunities to see Kristina Nolan ruffled."

"I'm not ruffled. I'm just irritated. And it's not relevant to the case. Paige is a different person than Ariana—"

"The ex-girlfriend's name is *Ariana?*" Lena was taking far too much pleasure in this. "She even has a sexy name!"

"Enough, Lena, please. It's not funny."

Her cousin's smile faded. "If I'm going to do this job for you, I have conditions. First, I want full transparency. No holding back information from me. If you or Hal know it, I know it."

Kristina nodded. "Of course. I mean, as long as we're within the bounds of attorney-client privilege."

"Second, I work my way. No shortcuts, no questionable tactics. None of Hal's dirty tricks."

Kristina hesitated. "There are gray areas, though. Sometimes you need to operate in them to win a case."

"Not me. I'm by-the-books, or I'm out."

"A cop was killed. The police won't play nice."

Lena's gaze hardened. "Kristina, this is not negotiable."

Kristina felt her jaw clench. But after a moment, she relented. "Okay. I'll make sure Hal understands."

"Good." Lena's expression softened slightly. "One more thing. When you guys get back on your feet, pay me what you can. I love you, but I also love not starving to death."

"Deal."

Lena thrust out her hand. As they shook, Kristina couldn't help wondering if she'd just made a deal that would cripple them at trial. But what other option did she have? Desperate people made desperate choices.

7

———

*N*EVER LET *them know they pushed your buttons.*

One of Hal's father's favorite sayings. As a kid, Hal used to imagine actual buttons—square red ones—being pushed in some NASA-like control room located inside his skull. And he'd always done his best to maintain the secrecy of the button-pushing.

But it wasn't always easy.

The moment he stepped inside the indoor shooting range, he broke out in a cold sweat. Even in the reception area, with a thick wall separating him from the firing lanes, the muffled pops of gunfire made his hands shake and shallowed his breathing. His hand moved instinctively to his right side, where he could trace the ridges of his scar through his dress shirt.

Inside his skull, a whole lot of buttons were being pushed right now.

"Are you okay?" There was a woman at the counter, watching him with evident concern.

"Fine." Hal willed the shaking to stop. He took a deep breath. By choosing this place as the location for their meeting, Detective Mateo Avalos—no friend of his—had definitely intended to push Hal's buttons. And Hal was determined not to let him see it. "Just meeting some people. Mateo Avalos and Wyatt Donovan."

The woman nodded. "They're just finishing up. You want to meet them in the lounge?"

Hal nodded and followed her through a door. There was an acrid gunpowder odor, and the smell almost stopped him in his tracks, wrenching buried memories from his mind.

The glint of metal as Oscar Hazenberg grabbed the deputy sheriff's gun.

The shouts and screams filling the courtroom, drowned a moment later by the blast.

Searing pain as he threw himself in front of Kristina.

The bullet had torn through his right lung and lodged in his spine, almost killing him. He'd survived, spent a lot of time in a wheelchair, even more time in physical therapy, and had miraculously emerged as his former self. At least, his former self with a nice, big helping of PTSD.

Detective Avalos knew all of this.

Never let them know they pushed your buttons.

"You sure you're okay?"

Hal forced a smile and straightened his tie. "All good."

"The lounge is right through that door."

He entered the lounge and found Avalos sitting at a hightop table with Donovan. A paper target was spread on the surface of the table, and they were hunched over it. The two made an unlikely pair—Wyatt Donovan, an assistant district attorney in an impeccably tailored suit, and Mateo Avalos in his worn leather jacket and jeans. Hal joined them, pasting on an expression of nonchalance.

"Slow Draw at Law," Hal said, clasping hands with Donovan. The assistant DA glared at him, as he always did when Hal used the nickname. Even though Donovan had been born and raised in Philly, he was called 'the Cowboy' in legal circles for no better reason than his first name was Wyatt. As in Wyatt Earp. It was a cringe-inducing nickname in Hal's opinion, made even cringier by the fact that Donovan had wholeheartedly embraced it, making it a part of his persona. That wasn't something Hal could simply let slide, so he'd given Donovan a more fitting name—'Slow Draw at Law'—and made sure to drive it home by trouncing him in every courtroom showdown. "Long time, no see, pardner."

"It has been a long time," Donovan said. "I assumed that's because your law firm went belly up." He smirked at Avalos.

"Not quite." Hal leaned between the two men, looking at the target. "What's this? Bonding over your shared love of Wild Wild West cosplay?"

Avalos stood up, turning on Hal with an angry glare. Hal stood his ground, but it wasn't easy. Avalos was only average height, but he had a kind of cop build that lent him a few extra inches by attitude alone. Broad shoulders filled out his leather jacket, which had enough scuffs and creases to look like armor rather than fashion. He glowered at Hal.

"Brave of you to show up here, Nolan. Thought you might still be … gun-shy."

"I'm many things, Avalos, but no one ever called me shy." *Never let them know they pushed your buttons.*

Donovan laughed, breaking the tension. "That's for sure."

"For your information," Avalos said, returning his attention to the table, "this is my target. You'll note the tight grouping of holes on the target's center mass, right here." Avalos pointed at the right side of the target's chest, where he'd consistently landed his shots, and Hal had to resist touching the same place on his own chest.

"Your marksmanship is impressively on-target, Detective."

Avalos grinned, until Hal added, "Too bad the same can't be said of your conviction rate."

"You trying to start something?"

"You're the one who insisted on meeting at a gun range."

"Hey, hey, Hal." Donovan got between them. "Relax, okay? I'm the one who proposed this place. I'm sorry—I wasn't thinking. I didn't do it intentionally."

Hal shook his head, incredulous. "Right. Because the DA's Office and Police Headquarters were unavailable."

"You actually think I'd let you into the DA's Office again after the stunt you pulled last year?" Donovan said. "Walking out with a copy of my opening statement under your arm? Listen, Mateo and I like to come here sometimes to blow off steam. It seemed like a convenient place. I forgot about what happened to you. I'm sorry."

Hal sighed. "Fine. Then let's get down to business. I'm here to discuss a plea deal for Paige Hess."

"A plea deal?" Avalos practically erupted.

"Paige claims she's innocent. But even assuming, for the sake of argument, that she really did run over this person, we're talking about an accident."

"*This person?*" Avalos glared at him. "Show some respect. This *person*, as you refer to him, was a cop. A detective. Landon Kirk."

Hal suppressed a smile. He'd come here knowing full well there would be no plea deal. In fact, a plea deal was the last thing he wanted. He wanted a trial and all of the juicy free publicity that would come with it. The only reason he'd proposed a meeting with Donovan and Avalos was to get information. And to do that, Hal needed to be the one pushing some buttons.

And he'd just pushed Avalos's, big-time.

"It doesn't matter if he was a detective."

"Maybe not to you."

Hal shrugged. "It doesn't change the fact that at worst this was a tragic car accident."

Donovan leaned back on his stool. "Come on, Nolan. The moment your client drove away, your 'accident' became a felony. There's no plea deal that's going to change that."

Hal turned to the prosecutor. "Why risk losing another trial to me when we can settle this reasonably?"

Donovan's face reddened. "Believe me, this case is as low-risk as they come."

"Really? Because I understand there were no eyewitnesses." Hal actually had no idea whether Donovan and Avalos had witnesses, and the curiosity was killing him.

"We don't need eyewitnesses," Donovan snapped. "We've got the damage to the front of your client's vehicle, consistent with an impact with a human body. We have her proximity to the location at the time of the incident. We have—" His voice cut off suddenly. "You're fishing, aren't you? That's what this meeting is really about."

"I don't fish," Hal scoffed. "I'm not a cowboy like you."

"Nice try, Nolan. You'll get what you're legally entitled to during discovery, not a word more."

A barrage of loud gunshots pounded from the shooting lanes. Without thinking, Hal dove for cover, crouching under the table. When the noise subsided, an overwhelming feeling of embarrassment washed over him. He had to force himself to rise from the floor.

Donovan had the decency to look away. Avalos didn't. "Flinch every time a car backfires, too, Nolan?"

The jab sent a surge of anger through him that no advice from his dad could control. "We can't all be as brave as you, hiding behind a badge."

Avalos's eyes flashed, and his voice was cold as he replied. "I saw your client's SUV myself, down at the impound lot. Forced myself to look at the damage where she smashed into him. Your client killed a cop. She's going down. And so are you. Finally."

Outside, Hal leaned against his car, taking deep breaths of cool air. The meeting hadn't been pleasant, but it hadn't been a total loss, either. He'd gotten a sneak preview of Donovan's and Avalos's evidence against Paige—evidence that sounded very circumstantial, and did not include any eye-witnesses.

He smiled grimly as he slid behind the wheel. Things were starting to look up. Now, he just needed to get his client out of jail.

8

———

THE PRELIMINARY ARRAIGNMENT courtroom was located in the basement of the Criminal Justice Center. With its recycled air, concrete walls, and lingering smell of sweat, it epitomized the unglamorous side of justice in Philadelphia. Hal couldn't be happier to be back.

He smiled and nodded at other lawyers they passed in the hallway—prosecutors and defense attorneys he hadn't seen in months. It felt like a homecoming.

"I checked the schedule and Beil's on the bench today," Kristina murmured as she matched his pace.

Hal tried not to groan. Although she would never admit it, Magistrate Judge Evelyn Beil held a strong bias in favor of law enforcement, almost always siding with the DA's Office. She also held an equally strong bias against Hal Nolan.

"Slow Draw must be bouncing in his saddle."

"Just stick to the facts and we should be okay," Kristina said. "And don't forget what happened at Quintana's bail hearing."

Beil had held him in contempt, and he'd spent the night in a jail cell. "Not an experience I'm likely to forget."

"Exactly. She's not charmed by your schtick."

Hal shot Kristina a look. "I don't have a *schtick*. My charm is genuine."

"Sure it is." Together, they pushed through the heavy doors and into the courtroom. Wyatt Donovan, already stationed at the prosecution table, looked up. His suit was perfectly pressed, his hair immaculate. Mateo Avalos was nowhere in sight—apparently bail hearings were beneath the detective.

Hal propped his briefcase on the defense table, then crossed the aisle to shake Donovan's hand. "You're early, Slow Draw. I didn't realize horses could travel so fast."

Donovan managed a tight smile. "I see you brought your babysitter," he said, gesturing at Kristina. "Maybe she'll keep you out of detention this time."

Before Hal could retort, he caught sight of Ariana Hess and his clever comeback died on his lips. She sat rigidly upright in the gallery, her hands moving restlessly in her lap, her lips pressed into a thin line. The sight of her like that brought back the seriousness of the moment.

Hal nodded to her, but her eyes were fixed on the video screen at the front of the room. The feed hadn't come to life yet, but it would soon show her sister Paige, piped in from a holding cell at the jail.

He took his place at the defense table beside Kristina. A moment later, Magistrate Judge Evelyn Beil entered, her no-nonsense demeanor drawing everyone's attention.

"All rise." The court officer's bellow filled the room.

The video screen flickered to life and Paige appeared, looking small and vulnerable. The dark circles under her eyes had gotten worse since their visit to the Philadelphia Industrial Correctional Center, and even on video Hal could see that she was shaking. Ariana's small sound of despair reached him from the gallery.

Magistrate Judge Beil's voice cut through the room. "We are

here for the preliminary arraignment of Paige Hess, who is charged with homicide by vehicle, including involuntary manslaughter as a lesser included charge, along with fleeing the scene of an accident involving death. Ms. Hess, do you understand the charges against you?"

Paige's voice came through tinny and distant. "Yes, Your Honor."

Hal took a step toward the judge's bench, eager to be heard, but the Cowboy beat him to it.

"Your Honor, the Commonwealth strongly opposes any consideration of bail in this case. Ms. Hess is accused of an odious crime—ramming a decorated police detective with her truck and leaving him to die in the street. She presents a clear danger to the community and a significant flight risk."

Hal felt his blood pressure rise. "Ramming? Really? And a Ford Explorer is not a truck—" The distinct sound of Kristina clearing her throat made him pause. "What I mean, Your Honor, is that Mr. Donovan's characterization of our client is inflammatory and unsupported by the facts. Ms. Hess has no prior criminal record. She poses no flight risk."

Beil's cold gaze fixed on Hal and seemed to pin him to the spot. "And what exactly do you propose, Mr. Nolan? That we simply release her on her own recognizance?"

"That would be great, if you're offering—"

"I'm not."

Hal felt Kristina's warning glance again. "Of course, Your Honor. We're simply asking for reasonable bail. Ms. Hess is presumed innocent, and she deserves the opportunity to assist in her own defense from outside a jail cell."

Donovan scoffed, earning a frosty look of his own from the magistrate judge.

"Something to add, Mr. Donovan?"

"Only to remind Your Honor that the defendant has already fled once—from the crime scene. I think that speaks volumes."

This time it was Hal who scoffed. "Ms. Hess has cooperated fully with the investigation. She voluntarily submitted to questioning by the police, and consented to a search of her vehicle. She did not flee from a crime scene—she denies ever being at a crime scene to begin with. She has significant ties to this community. She's lived in Philadelphia her entire life. She teaches at a local high school. And she has family here who can vouch for her character." He risked a glance at Ariana, watching silently. "Please, Your Honor."

Magistrate Judge Beil seemed to consider his words, her gaze flicking between him, Donovan, and the image of Paige on the screen. Hal held his breath.

"I'm inclined to grant bail," Beil said finally, raising a hand to silence Donovan's knee-jerk protest. "However, given the severity of the charges, I am setting such bail at $800,000."

"There's no way my client can afford that!" Hal said.

But Paige's face had already been replaced with that of the next defendant, and the courtroom was in motion as the magistrate judge turned to her next bail decision.

A flash of red hair caught Hal's attention as Ariana pushed past the few spectators, making her way toward him and Kristina. Even in distress, she moved in a way that brought back memories, her dress emphasizing a figure that still turned heads. But right now her striking green eyes were rimmed with red. "$800,000? Is there any way to lower that?" Her voice was tight. Her face looked on the verge of tears.

"Not at this stage," Hal said. "We can try to get it reduced later, but for now.... I'm sorry."

"What about a bail bondsman? Isn't that what people do in this situation?"

Hal nodded. "Yes, but a bail bondsman will require 10% down. That's still $80,000."

Ariana's jaw set. "I'll put up my condo."

Hal exchanged a quick glance with Kristina. "You could do that," he said, "but you need to understand the risks. You could lose your home if Paige violates any conditions of her release."

"She won't," Ariana cut him off. In a softer voice, she said, "Come on, Hal. You know Paige."

Hal nodded. "Okay. We'll start the paperwork."

In the basement hallway outside the courtroom, Hal watched as Ariana made a call, pacing nervously with her phone pressed to her ear. He thought of Paige, alone in her cell, pinning her hopes on them. He looked at Kristina, gnawing her lip with a worried look of her own. He knew exactly what she was thinking. How many people's livelihoods were they willing to put at risk?

Hal didn't know the answer. He only knew they needed to win.

9

———————

FADING daylight seeped through the grimy windows, casting shadows across their shabby office. Hal's tie hung loose around his neck. His shirtsleeves were rolled up. Kristina sat surrounded by piles of books. They'd managed to get Paige released on bail—by the skin of their teeth—and they both knew keeping her out of prison would take everything they had and then some.

So they were bouncing ideas off each other, using each other's brains, just like they'd tackled so many cases before. Their secret weapon—two minds that complemented each other, finding answers where others saw dead ends. It had worked in law school and it had carried their firm to the heights of the Philadelphia legal world. It would get them back to the top, too.

Assuming we win this case.

"The biggest problem is the Ford Explorer," Hal said. "We know the police towed it to an impound lot. We have to assume they had an accident reconstructionist work it over. At the shooting range, Donovan let slip that the damage to the front of the vehicle was consistent with an impact with a human body.

But if we can convince the trial judge to exclude evidence of the SUV—"

"On what basis?" Kristina looked up from a dog-eared legal text, a skeptical look in her eyes. They'd sold off most of their assets to cover the ransom, but she had not been able to part with her beloved legal tomes.

Hal paced. "Can we make a chain of custody argument? The cops only found the car because of a traffic stop, right? A cop pulled Paige over because he thought she was drunk. But she passed the sobriety test and the breathalyzer. If the traffic cop had no probable cause to pull her over, then anything he found —including the damage to the front of the SUV—is inadmissible. Fruit of the poisonous tree."

"That's not going to fly and you know it."

"Depends who gets assigned as our trial judge. There are a few who might buy that argument. And after getting Evelyn Biel for a magistrate judge at the bail hearing, we're due some good luck."

"You want to count on luck?" Kristina said. "All the traffic cop needs to do is testify that Paige was driving erratically, and he has enough probable cause for the stop. It's not a high bar."

Hal's jaw clenched. "Well, if we can't exclude the SUV, then we need to get our own expert into that impound lot to examine it."

"And how exactly are we going to afford an expert when you've so generously offered our services for free?"

"Let me worry about that."

She looked like she might argue, then shrugged. "Okay. I'll get to work on a pre-trial motion requesting access to the vehicle."

"Good. What else can we do?"

Kristina set aside the book and crossed the room to a battered whiteboard. "Let's make a timeline." The marker squeaked as she sketched out what they knew, her handwriting neat as always. Hal felt a twinge of sadness as he remembered their old office's sleek, state-of-the-art touchscreens, but there was something raw and immediate about Kristina's hand flowing across the whiteboard. No fancy graphics or digital wizardry—just the essentials, their ideas.

"It starts at a book club," she said, stepping back to survey her handiwork. "She had a glass of wine and drove home. The route took her past Foul Line. We've been there, by the way—good buffalo wings."

"I remember."

"Somewhere within five miles of Foul Line, a cop pulls her over because her driving looks erratic. He asks her to get out of the car, do some sobriety tests, take a breathalyzer—how long do you think all of that would take?"

Hal shook his head. "Fifteen minutes? Twenty?"

"And he notices the front of her car is damaged. She tells him she hit a deer a few days before—"

"It would be nice if we could confirm that," Hal said.

"I'll ask Lena to see what she can dig up. Maybe there was a witness, or a road crew cleared the mess." Her voice trailed off as she added more details to the whiteboard. "The cop lets her go, and she drives home to her apartment."

Hal moved behind his wife, close enough to catch the faint scent of her skin. He rested a hand on the small of her back. "Detective Dickwad arrives thirty minutes later with a warrant and a tow truck. That's an awful fast response time, even if the traffic cop called in about the damaged SUV minutes after letting Paige go."

Kristina turned, their faces inches apart. "Maybe we can work with that," she said. "Get the jury to believe the police jumped on the first possible suspect without doing any actual investigation."

"Knowing Avalos, I'm sure that's exactly what happened." Hal allowed himself a smile. "Guess we've still got a few tricks up our sleeves, huh?"

"Guess so."

His hands found her waist. The familiar curves of her body under his palms sent a thrill through him. "Have I ever told you how hot you look writing on a whiteboard? It's my weakness."

He felt more than heard Kristina's laugh. She tilted her head. "And here I thought it was my chest."

"That too," Hal admitted. Her skin was warm, soft. He pulled her closer, one hand sliding up to tangle in her hair. Kristina's arms wound around his neck, and her breasts, which were small and perfect and which he did indeed love, pressed against him. Their kiss started soft but quickly became more urgent.

And then Kristina stiffened in his arms. She pushed him away. Hal opened his eyes to find her glaring at him.

"Are you sure you wouldn't be more turned on by a cheerleader uniform?" Her voice held an edge that made Hal's stomach drop. A knot of guilt formed in his stomach, even though he knew he hadn't done anything wrong.

"Kristina, I told you, anything I had with Ariana is ancient history—"

"Maybe you should tell *her* that." Kristina's eyes flashed dangerously, but before she could say more, a sharp knock echoed through the office.

They stepped apart as Lena Randall marched inside, military-straight posture, observant eyes taking in the room—and them.

"If this is a bad time…"

"No, it's a perfect time." Kristina's voice slipped into a professional cadence. She took a step away from Hal and waved Lena toward the hodgepodge of chairs around the battered conference table. "What've you got for us? Good news?"

Lena's back remained straight, as if she'd come to a commanding officer to deliver a report, instead of her cousin. Her stiffness—present even at family gatherings—never ceased to unsettle Hal. "I visited Foul Line. It's an old-school dive bar in Fishtown, sticks out like a sore thumb with all the craft breweries and artisanal coffee shops around it."

"Good wings." Hal shot Kristina a smile. She didn't return it.

"I didn't eat," Lena said. "And I didn't learn much, either. Half the regulars couldn't tell you what they had for breakfast, much less what happened last week. But one name did keep surfacing. *Diego Messina*."

Hal struggled to hide the jolt of recognition, and he didn't dare look at Kristina. This was an interesting development, to say the least.

Lena proceeded to paint a picture of Messina—they didn't need her to, but she didn't know that. Lena's description was spot-on. Handsome, impeccably dressed, early forties, a mobster of the old school. "He's a regular at Foul Line, likes to hold court there. And he was there that night."

Hal felt the excitement building in his chest, but he managed to keep his voice level. "Did you learn anything else?"

"Tried to. I reached out to a couple of contacts I have in law enforcement, but they stonewalled me after I mentioned your names."

"Wait—you mentioned our names?" Hal said. "Why would you do that? You know we're not exactly on the Christmas card list at Police HQ."

"Because, as I told Kristina, I do this my way or not at all. Is that a problem?" She leveled a stare at him.

"No, no problem." And it was true—for now. He might not approve of Lena Randall's methods, but the woman had just brought them gold.

He glanced at Kristina, but she avoided his gaze.

Lena looked from one of them to the other. "Is everything ... okay here?"

"Yes, fine," Hal said quickly. "Lena, we'd also like you to look into Paige's story about hitting the deer. See if you can find something to back it up in court."

"On it."

Lena rose from her chair. The moment she left the office, Hal turned to face Kristina. The earlier tension about Ariana was still unresolved, but a new one had eclipsed it.

"I know what you're thinking...."

"Then you know I'm thinking this is an ethical line we can't cross."

"Come on, Kristina. Diego Messina being at Foul Line that night? It's better than anything we could have hoped for Lena to find." Landon Kirk was a detective. Diego Messina was a known organized crime figure. It stood to reason that Messina had been behind Kirk's death, not some random high school teacher. Maybe Kirk had been investigating Messina, and Messina killed him. It was a good story—exactly the kind that juries loved. There was only one small ethical problem.

"Diego Messina," Kristina said icily, "is our client."

10

―――――

HAL'S MIND raced as he prowled the cramped office. Lena had just handed them the break they'd been praying for, a viable alternative to the DA's theory of the case, a criminal just as likely, if not more so, to have been the cause of Landon Kirk's death than Paige Hess. He could already see the headlines, the rush of new clients that would follow a win like this. And Kristina was worried about crossing lines?

Her angry glare tracked him as he paced. "Hal, sit down."

Her stern expression, usually endearing, now sent a bolt of irritation through him. He knew it meant a lecture was coming.

"We can't use this," she said. "There are rules—rules even you have to respect. Diego Messina is a client."

Hal felt a wave of frustration. "He *was* a client, Kristina. *Past tense.* He abandoned us after the ransomware attack, just like all the rest of our fair-weather retainers."

"Not in any formal way. He never officially terminated the relationship."

"Listen to you. You sound like Lena." Hal's jaw clenched.

"No, I sound like a lawyer who actually paid attention during our Professional Responsibility class."

She was never going to let that go, was she? "I would have aced that course if the classes weren't at 9 in the morning. What kind of student gets up for 9 AM classes?"

"I got up."

"Yeah, well." He waved a hand. "My point."

Kristina stared at him, not amused. "Creating reasonable doubt about Paige's guilt by suggesting Diego Messina killed Landon Kirk would breach our duty of loyalty. It would violate the attorney-client privilege. It would be a major conflict of interest. We could be disbarred."

"So what would you suggest?" he asked, unable to keep his voice from rising. "What's the ethical solution? Please, Kristina, enlighten me with your vaunted legal brilliance!"

She endured his tirade with a steady gaze. "We need to withdraw from representing Paige."

The words hit him like a physical blow. He collapsed into the closest chair. Withdraw? Give up their best chance at a comeback? Hand a sure-win to some other defense attorney? The very thought made his skin crawl. He could already picture the smug looks of Donovan and Avalos and everyone else who'd been waiting for The Nolan Law Firm to fail.

"You can't be serious," he muttered, his voice barely above a whisper. "This case is our lifeline. Without it, we're toast."

"Hal, that's not true."

"We'll be defending public urinators until we run out of money."

"We can't compromise our integrity."

"Our integrity!" He spat the words. "Our integrity is what got us into this mess!"

"No, a cybercriminal got us into this mess. Our integrity will be what gets us out."

They held each other's gazes for a moment, then Hal broke

eye-contact, shaking his head. "No, Kristina, I'm sorry. That's just ... it's bullshit."

She crossed her arms over her chest. "Then explain why it's bullshit, Hal. Enlighten *me* with *your* vaunted legal brilliance."

Hal leaned forward. "Okay, I will. Messina doesn't qualify as a client anymore. He ghosted us. No communication, no payments, no contact of any kind for months. Any reasonable interpretation of the rules would say our duty of loyalty ended when he walked away."

Kristina's brow furrowed, but Hal pressed on before she could interrupt. "And as for attorney-client privilege—which, yes, I know you're going to say extends past the end of the relationship—we simply won't use any confidential information. We won't need to."

An incredulous scoff escaped Kristina's lips, but her lack of an actual comeback encouraged him. "Think about it," he said. "We only need to present two facts. One, Messina, a known crime figure, was at the bar that night. Any of the regulars Lena talked to at Foul Line can testify to that. And two, Landon Kirk was a detective. That's a fact that will already be in evidence."

"You skipped one. Who's going to testify that Messina's a criminal?"

"We'll find a way to get his criminal record in. Public records, nothing confidential."

He watched the wheels turning behind Kristina's eyes. Her defensive posture began to soften, if only slightly.

"We're not revealing anything Messina told us in confidence," Hal said. "We're just connecting dots that are already out there in the open. It's not our fault if those dots happen to establish reasonable doubt for Paige Hess."

"And throw our former client under the bus. I don't know, Hal," she said, but her voice lacked its earlier conviction, and he noted her use of the term *former client*. "It's a creative interpretation of the rules of professional conduct."

"Well, that is my specialty."

He held his breath, watching the internal struggle play out across her face. Finally, she let out a long sigh.

"Alright," she said. "But we stick to those three facts. Nothing else. Nothing Messina confided in us when we were his attorneys."

"Wouldn't dream of it."

"I'm serious, Hal."

"I know." He felt a grin spread across his face. "Now let's get to work. We've got a trial to win."

11

_____

NIGHT HAD FALLEN when they finally pushed through the heavy fire door into the alley behind the building, ready to head home. The air was cool, but it carried the stench of rotting garbage that seemed to cling to their new office building. Hal tried to hold his breath as they headed toward their battered old Camry.

Only a single, dim streetlight at the far end of the alley lit their way. If the darkness wasn't enough to make him uneasy, the distant wail of sirens was another reminder that they were no longer working in the swanky part of town.

"Watch your step," Hal muttered, more out of a desire to hear his own voice than necessity—Kristina was as familiar with this plot of urban decay as he was.

"Easier said than done."

As if to prove her point, Hal's shoe squelched over a rotting mound of discarded fast-food.

"Remind me to take my shoes off _before_ we go inside our apartment."

The Camry waited near the mouth of the alley. Hal reached for the door handle. His fingers grazed cool metal.

He sensed movement behind him in the split-second before hell broke loose.

A shadow rushed from the darkness, impossibly fast. There was no time to react, no chance to warn Kristina. A blur of motion barreled toward him. He didn't identify it as a fist until it connected with his jaw and sent him sprawling.

His head cracked against the filthy pavement with an explosion of pain. Blood filled his mouth. The world swam out of focus, his vision clouding. He blinked furiously, desperate to clear his head.

"Hal!"

Kristina's cry sliced through the haze of pain, but was cut short in a strangled gasp. The sound chilled him to his core.

He fought the dizziness and clawed his way upright. His legs wobbled. Nausea churned in his stomach, threatening to overwhelm him.

The man was dressed all in black, including gloves and a ski mask that obscured his face. One arm crushed Kristina to his chest, pinning her arms. His other hand pressed a knife to her throat.

Hal's heart stopped.

The blade gleamed dully in the meager light, its edge already drawing a thin line of blood across Kristina's pale skin. Hal could see the rapid rise and fall of her chest, hear the slight tremor in her breathing. Her eyes were wide with horror.

"Wait!" The word tore from Hal's throat, a desperate rasp. His hands rose, trembling. "Just take our wallets. We won't resist. You don't need to hurt—"

"I don't want your money, lawyer."

"Okay. That's okay." Hal's gaze was riveted to the knife, to Kristina's straining neck. "Tell us what you do want—"

The tip of the knife nipped into the skin of Kristina's neck.

Blood pooled around it. Kristina's eyes filled with tears. "What I want right now is for you to shut up."

"Hurt her again and I swear...." Hal's voice hardened.

A chuckle sounded from behind the mask. "A lawyer and a tough guy."

"You really want to find out?"

The man pulled the knife away from Kristina's neck, but kept it ready, about an inch away. The spot where the tip had pierced her skin was visible, a long trickle of blood sliding down into her collar. She breathed hard, sobbing.

"Lose the trial," the man said.

Hal swallow. "Which trial?"

"Don't mess with me."

"Not the public urinator, I'm guessing—" The knife surged toward Kristina's throat. "Okay, okay!"

"Hess goes down, or you do. Understand?"

"Why? Who are you?"

"Goodbye, lawyer."

The attack ended as quickly as it had begun. The masked man shoved Kristina to the ground, her knees hitting the pavement with enough force to make a sound. Hal rushed to her, his hands shaking as he helped her up.

"Kristina?"

"I'm okay."

He pulled her close, feeling her body trembling. The alley had gone silent except for the sound of their ragged breathing.

"Are you sure?" He checked her throat, her body.

"Hal, I'm okay."

He fumbled his phone from his pocket. "We need the police." He started to call 911. Before he could finish, Kristina gripped his wrist. He looked at her, startled.

"Think," she said, her voice a whisper. "Someone attacked us. Someone violent who wants Paige to be found guilty."

"Yeah, I'm aware—"

"Hal." She forced him to meet her gaze. "This had to be Diego Messina."

"We don't know that."

"Lena's been asking questions about him—at Foul Line, to the police. You think a man like Diego Messina wants to be dragged into a murder trial? And who else would threaten us? Who else stands to benefit?"

"Fine. Then I'll tell the police—"

Her grip tightened on his wrist. "Diego threatening us supports your theory. But if you call 911, we lose the element of surprise." Her voice was firm, her gaze intense. "Better to expose it in court. Donovan and Avalos won't know what hit them."

Hal shook his head. "The guy put a knife to your throat. What if he comes back? We'd be taking a huge risk."

"And when has that ever stopped you?"

"When it puts you in danger."

Kristina leaned against him. "You said yourself, we need to win this one. Are you going to let a thug in a mask stop us?"

Hal hesitated, then lowered his phone. "I guess not."

12

———————

EVEN THREE DAYS LATER, a wave of pain pulsed through Hal's bruised chin as he shaved. He splashed cold water on his face and winced, catching Kristina's gaze in the mirror's reflection. She stood in the bathroom doorway, arms crossed, her neck bearing two faint bruises. The sight of her injuries made his jaw clench.

She held up her phone. "Judge Booker granted my pre-trial motion for access to the Ford Explorer."

"I never doubted you."

"Catching Booker was a lucky break."

"Told you we were due one."

The Honorable Judge Solomon Booker might not be the most defense-friendly judge on the bench—despite the fact that he'd spent over a decade as a public defender—but he was meticulously focused on precise legal precedent and ran his courtroom like a law school from hell. In other words, the perfect judge for a law nerd like Kristina.

"Now we just need an expert," Kristina said.

"Already have one. Desmond Cobb."

"What?" The warmth drained from Kristina's face. "You didn't even ask me? Consult me?"

"I told you I'd take care of it."

"But *Desmond Cobb?*"

"We should get over there ASAP." Hal rubbed aftershave into his cheeks and washed his hands. "I'll ask Desmond if he can meet me at the impound lot today."

"*You?* Not us?" She managed to look even angrier.

He dried his hands on a towel, avoiding her gaze. "I thought, you know, it would be better if you stay home where it's safe. And I know how you feel about Desmond—"

"Which is why you didn't mention him until now."

"Kristina—"

"It's my case, too. I'm going."

He turned to face her, could tell from the intensity of her stare that this argument was not winnable. "I'll drive."

The trip to the police impound lot was short but tense. Kristina hadn't spoken since they'd left the apartment, and Hal recognized the distant look in her eyes that meant she was brooding.

"What is it?"

She frowned, watching the passing buildings. "Judge Booker is strict. He's going to require us to qualify Desmond Cobb as an expert. Did you think about that?"

"Desmond *is* an expert. He knows cars, knows accidents."

"He knows fraud, Hal."

"And?" They'd defended Desmond Cobb on insurance fraud charges a few years back, but that was exactly what made him perfect for Paige's trial. Who better to spot inconsistencies in the testimony of the accident reconstructionist than a man who knew every trick?

"You don't think Donovan is going to impeach him with that?" Kristina said.

"He can try. But we got Desmond acquitted. Legally speaking, he never committed fraud."

A humorless laugh escaped Kristina's lips. "Legally speaking."

"Look," Hal said, "in an ideal world, we'd have our pick of respectable experts. But we have no operating capital. *None.* Desmond's willing to do us a favor, just like your cousin."

"So now you're comparing Lena to a fraudster?"

"Actually, maybe we should set them up. Lena could learn a few tricks." He grinned at the thought.

"That's not funny."

"Bottom line, the Ford Explorer is a problem. We need to deal with it. Desmond is our best option."

Kristina turned back to the window. "Just remember I warned you."

Finally they reached the police impound lot. Chain-linked fences surrounded a graveyard of vehicles. Hal parked in the visitor lot and exchanged a quick look with Kristina before they both climbed out of the car. Odors of oil and rust filled his nostrils.

He spotted Desmond Cobb leaning against a gleaming Mercedes. The man straightened as they approached, his suit straining against his paunch.

"What the hell are you driving?" Desmond said, looking past them to the Camry. "You may as well leave that thing here—it will fit right in with the other wrecks."

"Nice to see you, too."

"Sorry. I'm a car guy. It bothers me."

"It's temporary," Hal said. He forced a smile, aware of Kristina's stiffening posture beside him. "Thanks for doing this, Desmond. I—*we*—appreciate it."

"You kidding me? Pass up a chance to help my favorite legal dream team?" Desmond's gaze flicked to Kristina and his smile faltered. "Besides, it's not every day you get to poke around a car that took out a cop, am I right?"

Hal winced, painfully aware of Kristina's darkening mood. "The car hit a *deer*," Hal said quickly, "according to our client."

"Of course it did."

A stern-faced officer emerged from a booth, his hand resting casually on his holstered weapon. His eyes, hard and unforgiving, swept over their small group before settling on Hal. "This is a restricted area."

"We have a court order," Kristina said. She flourished the document from Judge Booker.

The officer snatched it from her. "Wait here." He disappeared back into the booth. Through the window, Hal could see him making a call.

Desmond snorted. "I don't think he likes you, Kristina."

Kristina shrugged. "We're not here to be liked."

"Enemy territory," Hal agreed. "Here he comes. Good boy."

The officer returned, his frown deepening into barely contained hostility. "You have one hour. I'll be observing the entire time to ensure protocol is followed."

"What, you don't trust us?" Hal said.

The guard didn't answer. They followed him through the impound lot. Police officers and technicians moved about with purposeful efficiency, a few casting suspicious looks in their direction as they passed. Eventually, they reached Paige's Ford Explorer.

Hal saw the damage to the front of the vehicle and felt his stomach tighten.

Desmond whistled. He circled the SUV, examining it with the practiced eye of someone who'd seen his fair share of accident scenes—legitimate and staged.

Hal joined him where he crouched by the front bumper. "What do you think?" Hal said, pitching his voice low.

"I can work with it," Desmond said.

Hal ran a finger along the wreckage of the bumper. "Could this have been caused by a deer?"

"Could be a fucking llama if that's what you want it to be."

"Are you sure?" Hal said, aware of Kristina's skeptical gaze boring into his back. "Don't just tell me what I want to hear. You're going to be cross-examined."

Desmond stood, brushing dirt from his pants. "Look, something big and solid did this. But was it a detective or Bambi? Nobody can say for sure." He shrugged. "Lots of room for interpretation."

Hal nodded. "Sounds like reasonable doubt to me."

He glanced at Kristina, saw the tightness around her eyes. She met his gaze, then looked away.

"Don't worry, I'll deliver on the stand," Desmond said. "By the time I'm done with their accident reconstructionist, he won't be able to get a job at Jiffy Lube."

Hal grinned, already imagining Donovan's expression. He doubted the Cowboy had ever faced a witness quite like Desmond Cobb. He clapped the man on the shoulder. "Thanks, Desmond. We'll be in touch with next steps."

The drive back to the office was quiet until Hal couldn't stand it anymore. "I know you're not happy about this."

"A *llama*?"

"You heard that part?"

"I heard all of it, Hal."

He felt his face redden. "Desmond's sense of humor can be—"

Kristina held up a hand, cutting him off. "He seems like he knows what he's talking about. Let's just…. Let's make it work. Make sure he's professional on the stand."

"We can prep him together." Hal felt a sudden giddiness wash over him—the horror of the alleyway attack fading for the first time. "I think we're actually going to win this. Between throwing the blame on Messina—"

"Our former client," Kristina put in.

"And putting Desmond on the stand to testify that Paige's Ford Explorer wasn't involved—"

"The testimony of a criminal."

"And introducing evidence that someone threatened us to make sure Paige takes the fall—"

"Which we didn't report to the police."

Hal grinned at her. "We're about to knock the Cowboy off his high horse."

A brief, sardonic smile played at the corners of Kristina's mouth, telling him they were on the same page even if she wasn't ready to admit it.

They had a plan, a solid defense strategy.

Now all they had to do was live long enough to sell it to the jury.

13

———

THE HOMICIDE UNIT was the most prestigious division in the Philadelphia District Attorney's Office, a place where careers were made and broken. Currently ruled with an iron fist by Aldo Burke, the unit had delivered an unprecedented series of court-room victories—and with each win, the pressure only increased.

Approaching Burke's office for a status meeting on the Paige Hess case, Donovan turned the corner and saw Samantha Klein leaving. He felt a stab of dread at the sight of her. Sam was a homicide prosecutor like him—but wouldn't be for long. Burke didn't tolerate mistakes, and after she'd made one, Sam had become a pariah, relegated to the lowest, easiest cases—death by a thousand plea deals.

As she brushed past him, she moved like a wounded animal, head down, retreating. Watching her go, Donovan realized he was holding his breath.

Won't happen to me. I'm not like her. I'm the fucking Cowboy.

Donovan adjusted his tie, smoothed back his already-perfect hair. Unlike Sam Klein, he didn't make mistakes. He could handle the pressure. He delivered victories.

He found Burke behind his desk, bushy eyebrows furrowed

as he studied a case file. Burke didn't look up when Donovan entered, just gestured toward the chair across from him.

"You wanted to see me about the Hess case?" Donovan kept his tone carefully neutral. His pulse quickened—they'd only recently had a judge assigned and had not even impaneled a jury yet. Burke didn't usually take such an early interest in a trial.

Burke finally met his gaze. "I want to make sure you grasp the importance of this case."

Ah, so that explained Burke's interest. The entire police department would be watching this one, exerting as much influence as possible to see justice served. "I understand. Officer down cases are always high profile."

Burke watched him coldly. "This isn't about the dead cop."

Donovan felt the ground shift under him. "It isn't?"

"The Nolans have been a stain on this city's justice system for too long. Running their little circus act, turning proceedings into sideshows." His hand tightened on the file. "They're on their last legs, but this trial could bring them back. I want them crushed. Permanently."

Donovan leaned back, considering. Burke's hatred of the Nolans went back years, to when they'd humiliated him in the Davion Blake case—delaying, but not preventing, his ascendance to head of the Homicide Unit.

"Rumor is the Nolans are close with the Queen B herself," Donovan said, referring to the DA. Her friendship with Hal and Kristina Nolan was an open secret.

Burke's eyebrows shot up in contempt. "All the more reason to question her judgment." He tossed the file onto his desk. "Don't worry about Jessie Black. Can you handle this or not?"

Donovan felt a smile spread across his face. A chance to put Hal Nolan in his place, to wipe that smug grin off his face, to never hear "Slow Draw at Law" whispered in the courthouse hallways again?

"Consider it done."

The bushy eyebrows settled back into their natural scowl. "Don't get cocky. The Nolans are like cockroaches—they always find a way to survive. Better prosecutors than you have tried to stomp on them only to end up flat on their backs."

Prosecutors like you, Donovan thought but didn't say. "We have a strong case. And Detective Avalos hates them as much as you do." He smiled. "Maybe more."

Burke's expression hardened. "Avalos is a hothead. One cross-examination from Hal Nolan, and he'll explode on the stand."

Donovan felt a flicker of defensiveness—Mateo was a friend, and a thorough, diligent detective—but he didn't dare contradict Burke. "I'll control him."

"Keep him off the stand."

"But he's the lead detective—"

Burke's eyes darkened. "Are you questioning me, Wyatt?"

"No, sir."

"Do not let Avalos anywhere near the witness stand."

"Got it." Donovan stood, smoothing his suit jacket. He had work to do, witnesses to prep, a strategy to perfect. This time, Hal and Kristina wouldn't know what hit them until it was too late.

14

———

In criminal trials, discovery was the prosecution's reluctant gift to the defense—a present wrapped in red tape and surrendered with the grace of a toddler forced to share candy. The rules of criminal procedure required the prosecution to divulge all relevant evidence to the defense before trial—a rule that did not go both ways—and any competent defense attorney exploited this tiny advantage to the fullest.

Hal considered himself a very competent defense attorney.

Of course, prosecutors had strategies for mitigating the obligation, one favorite old standby being to hide the good stuff in box-loads of useless paper. Anticipating Donovan's slavish devotion to the DA's Office's playbook, Hal rented a van and a cart, and brought Lena and her Marine Corps muscles along for the heavy lifting.

He parked the van outside the DA's Office. The Widener Building loomed before them. Sunlight gleamed on its stone facade, highlighting the arched windows, decorative columns, and intricate detailing around the roofline. Some people considered the building an architectural treasure. Hal considered it a gaudy monument to bureaucratic self-importance, designed by someone who'd had too much time on their hands back in 1914.

Kristina hopped down from the van's passenger seat. Before Lena could climb out of the back, Hal turned in his seat to catch her eye. "Find anything about the masked man?"

She shook her head. "The attack should be a police matter, Hal. You should—"

"We already explained this. If we go to the police, Detective Avalos will learn about it. He'll tell Donovan, and the two of them will find a way to neutralize it before we can spring it on them in court. This needs to stay between the three of us for now."

"Well then you're asking for a miracle."

Hal sighed. "You delivered Diego Messina. So far your miracle rate is pretty good. How about the deer?"

"Nothing. No police or road crew response, no camera footage.... I found a secluded stretch of road near Foul Line. If Paige hit a deer, she must have done it there."

"We could really use a witness. Stay on it, okay?"

Lena nodded before getting out of the van.

Hal's heart rate rose as the three of them navigated the halls of the DA's Office, where they were clearly *personae non gratae*. Angry, suspicious looks were the order of the day, and the cart's squeaky wheels announced their presence like an out-of-tune violin.

Donovan's door swung open before Hal could knock. The prosecutor looked the three of them over with even more disdain than usual. "Think you could make even more noise? People are trying to work here. Classy as ever, Nolan."

"No need to get your spurs in a twist, Slow Draw. Or should we call Judge Booker and let him know you're not in the mood to share the discovery materials?"

Donovan gave an exasperated shake of his head as he pulled

the door wider, revealing a stack of boxes in the corner of his office—predictable as ever. "All yours."

Hal brushed past him to grab the first box. He grunted, staggering under its unexpected weight. Lena hurried in to help him.

"What's the matter, Nolan?" Donovan's eyes glittered with amusement. "Had to cancel your gym membership to make rent?"

"Did you load these boxes with the weight of your ego?"

"Nope. Just the weight of the evidence that's going to bury your client."

Hal shook his head. He hadn't thought it possible, but Slow Draw seemed even more snide than usual. What had gotten into the man? "Sorry to break it to you, Wyatt, but the Commonwealth's case isn't as airtight as you think."

"Oh?" Donovan's voice rose with mock curiosity. "Are you referring to this silly Diego Messina angle your investigator has been pursuing?"

Hal's eyes darted to Lena's across the box they both held. Talk about an *I told you so* moment. Hal wished he could take some satisfaction in it. At least Lena had the grace to look abashed, turning her head away.

Donovan's laugh was sharp and unpleasant. "A mob hit? That's the best theory the great Hal and Kristina Nolan could come up with? I expected better."

Hal kept his tone light. "We're just following the evidence. You and Avalos should give it a try sometime."

"Mateo and I live for evidence. In fact, let me give you a sneak-peek of what's inside those boxes. It's the least I can do, since your investigator has been so forthcoming with the police." Donovan's earlier amusement hardened into something predatory. "Your client and the victim knew each other."

The words landed like hammer blows. "That's ridiculous," Hal bit out.

Donovan crossed his arms. "It's the truth. And it means this was no random hit-and-run. It was intentional. Paige Hess aimed her car at Landon Kirk. Forget vehicular homicide. This was murder."

Hal felt the world tilt. His magnificent defense strategy was crumbling in real time. He tried to keep his face neutral as Donovan watched him closely, seeming to lap up his panic.

"One more thing, Hal." He leaned against his desk, savoring the moment. "We're going for the death penalty."

Hal didn't need to ask who "we" meant. The presence of Aldo Burke might as well have been in the room with them.

"Not looking so arrogant now, are you?" Donovan said. "Have fun with the discovery materials."

The trip outside was tense and silent as they wheeled the loaded cart to the van. It wasn't until he was safely ensconced behind the wheel, the boxes of discovery crammed into the back, that Hal dared to speak.

"This is why honesty is not always the best policy, Lena." He gripped the steering wheel until his knuckles turned white.

"I had to disclose who I was working for—"

"No, you really didn't."

"We have bigger problems than Donovan knowing about Messina." Kristina's voice was tight. "If Paige and Kirk really knew each other, our entire defense strategy needs to be reworked."

"Reworked? It's shot to hell." Hal slammed his palm against the hard plastic steering wheel. "You were supposed to be investigating Paige's story, Lena. How did you miss that she knew Kirk?"

Lena's eyes flashed with frustration. "Paige never mentioned knowing him. And she had no reason to hide anything from us, so I just trusted—"

"Trusted? Where did you get your investigator's license, a gumball machine outside Police HQ?"

"I'll get on it right away," Lena said from the backseat, her voice clipped.

"You better. The trial's coming up fast. We need that information yesterday."

He pulled out of their space and into Philadelphia traffic, the load of boxes in the back weighing the van like an anchor.

"Well," Kristina said, "you wanted a murder case. Now we have one."

He shot her a look. "We need to go through those discovery materials with a fine-tooth comb. Look for any inconsistencies, any holes in Donovan's case."

"I'll start as soon as we unload."

"And I'll join you," Hal said, "but first I'm going to have a little heart-to-heart with our client."

15

———

Hal rapped sharply on Paige Hess's door. His anger had only gotten stronger during his drive to her apartment building. Now, as he heard soft footsteps and the click of a deadbolt disengaging, he was vibrating with frustration. Paige's face appeared surprised to see him.

"Is something wrong?"

Hal pushed past her into the small apartment. "We need to talk."

"Shouldn't we meet at your office?" Paige closed the door, then turned to look at him. Apprehension flitted across her face. "Did something happen with my case?"

Hal tore his gaze away from her, taking in the apartment. The small living room was neat but sparse. Her worn furniture looked like it had probably been bought secondhand. Bookshelves lined one wall, crammed with paperbacks and school textbooks and a mug with *#1 Teacher* printed on it in flowing script. On the coffee table, he saw a stack of what appeared to be half-graded papers. He noted the date at the top of the first sheet —a date just days before her arrest. Before her life had exploded. He supposed her class had a new teacher now, or at least a substitute.

The thought tugged at something within him, softening his anger—but only slightly.

"Hal, what is it?"

He turned to face her. "I just had an interesting chat with Wyatt Donovan. He seems pretty confident that you and Landon Kirk weren't strangers. He has evidence you knew each other."

Paige's face paled, and she sank onto the couch. "What kind of evidence?"

"So it's true?" Hal paced the small living room, then came to a stop in front of her. "I'm only going to ask this once, and you better tell me the truth, Paige. What exactly was your relationship?"

"We were acquaintances. That's all."

"Acquaintances." Hal barked out a laugh that made Paige flinch. "How did you know him? When did you meet?"

Paige avoided his gaze. Her fingers twisted the hem of her shirt. "He ran a safety training exercise at my school six months ago. What to do in case of an active shooter. We ... we talked afterward. He seemed nice."

Hal rubbed a hand over his face. "And?"

"If you're implying we had some torrid romance, we didn't. Landon's married, and I'm ... I'm hardly someone he would notice even if he was single. We stayed in touch. Nothing serious. We'd text occasionally, meet for coffee. He was ... he was nice to me. Listened when I needed someone to talk to."

Her story was strange, but Hal had found that his clients' strangest stories usually turned out to be the truest ones. He dropped onto the couch with a frustrated sigh. "Why didn't you tell us this? Do you have any idea how it looks—you knowing the man you're being accused of running down in the street? I'm supposed to face a jury and tell them this is all just a big coincidence?"

Paige's eyes filled with tears. "That's why I didn't tell you. I know how it looks. But I didn't kill him, Hal."

He studied her face. If there were signs of deception, he didn't see them. All he saw was fear and desperation and sadness. "Now Donovan's claiming you hit Kirk on purpose. He's revised the charges to include first degree murder. He's going for the death penalty."

Paige's hand flew to her mouth. "He can do that?"

"He can and he is."

A low keening sound escaped her as she doubled over, wrapping her arms around herself. "Oh God." Her body shook. "They're going to kill me. They're going to kill me for something I didn't do."

Looking at her—this woman who'd never tried a beer in high school—Hal felt what remained of his anger fade away. She was innocent, but proving it to a jury....

"Donovan hasn't seen our full hand yet. We still have some surprises." Hal thought of Desmond Cobb's testimony and the masked man who'd threatened his and Kristina's lives. "We can still win this, Paige."

She nodded, tears streaming down her face. "I'm so sorry, Hal. I never meant to hide anything.... I didn't think."

"Just don't hold anything else back, okay? Kristina and I are your lawyers, but we can't help you unless we know everything. Jury selection begins in a few days. We can't afford any more surprises."

"I understand. There won't be any."

Hal stood up and walked to the door. "I need you to write down every interaction you had with Kirk. Times, dates, and locations, no matter how insignificant. We need to get ahead of this."

"I'll do it right away."

He stepped into the hallway, closed the door behind him, and made his way to the fire stairs. This was not a disaster. He and Kristina would need to restructure their defense strategy, but most of it should still be salvageable.

He was lost in thought when he reached the bottom of the stairwell and a strong hand gripped his arm, spinning him around and slamming him against the wall.

His heart jumped into his throat as he braced himself for a repeat of the attack from a few nights ago. But it wasn't a masked man this time.

"Diego," he said.

Diego Messina glared at him in the gloom of the stairwell. Then he let go of Hal and tugged the lapels of his expensive suit into place. "Never figured you for the backstabbing type," he said, his voice filled with scorn.

"And I never figured you for the type who would send a goon to put a knife to my wife's throat."

"What the hell are you talking about?" The confusion that flashed across Messina's face looked genuine enough, but Hal didn't buy it. Messina had been born and raised in the mob. Lying was second nature to him. And as Kristina had pointed out, who else stood to benefit from Paige losing her trial?

"I know what you're planning, Hal. To put regulars from Foul Line on the stand at this teacher's trial, make me out to be a killer."

Hal let out a bitter laugh. "Honestly, I expected a little more sophistication from you." He fixed his own rumpled jacket.

"What's that supposed to mean?"

"It's a trial strategy, Diego. You were at the bar that night. Showing that to the jury helps create reasonable doubt for my client. But it doesn't mean you'll be charged for the crime. You probably won't be—"

"Probably?"

"You're a mob underboss. If there was evidence against you, don't you think the police would have acted on it? The PPD would love to take you down. Instead, they arrested some teacher. Doesn't that tell you something?"

"You're such a good bullshitter, Hal. Listen to me very carefully. I'm not going to be your patsy. You think anyone will testify that I was at Foul Line that night? Think again. No one remembers a thing."

"My investigator has statements. I can call those people as hostile witnesses if I need to, impeach them."

Messina's face twisted with barely controlled rage. "Do that, and I will destroy you. You and Kristina."

Hal felt a cold sweat break out on his forehead. "Diego, come on. Paige Hess is our client. We need to advocate for her, just like we used to advocate for you, before you dumped us."

"Is that what this is really about? I hurt your feelings?" Messina's laugh was harsh and humorless. With a violent shove, he thrust open the exit door. "Remember what I said, Hal, because I meant every word of it."

Then he was gone, the door slamming shut behind him with a heavy clang.

Hal leaned against the wall and let out a ragged breath. He'd thought things couldn't get worse after Donovan's latest revelation. Apparently, he'd been wrong.

16

———

Kristina's eyes fluttered open, her mind instantly registering the absence of Hal's warmth beside her. She glanced at the bedside clock. 2:37 AM. A tapping noise reached her from beyond the bedroom.

With a sigh, she swung her legs over the edge of the bed and headed for the doorway, following a faint glow from the other room.

She found Hal in the darkened kitchenette, his face lit by his laptop screen. His fingers were busy on the keyboard. Scattered papers surrounded him, along with a half-empty glass of water.

"What are you doing up?" Her voice was thick with sleep. She picked up his glass and drank the rest of the water.

"Couldn't sleep, so I decided to do some research for tomorrow."

Kristina peered over his shoulder, trying to make sense of the jumble of open tabs and documents. "Are those...."

"Car accident reports, DUIs, and traffic violations." A hint of excitement crept into his voice. "I'm checking every name from the prospective juror list."

A knot formed in Kristina's stomach. "Hal—"

Hal turned to face her, a familiar gleam in his eye. "We want to pack this jury with as many crappy drivers and drunks as possible. People who've been in accidents, who don't worry about having a few too many before getting behind the wheel. We don't want saints. We want people who will look at Paige and think, 'There but for the grace of God go I.' I've already found a few good prospects."

Kristina pinched the bridge of her nose, feeling a headache forming. "Hal, I thought I was handling jury selection."

"You are," he said quickly. "I'm just helping."

"This isn't helping." Kristina took a deep breath, trying to soften her tone. "The goal is an impartial jury. A jury of Paige's peers. You know we need to be careful with Judge Booker. He doesn't tolerate shenanigans."

"Shenanigans? This is all public information. It's not like I'm hacking the Pentagon here."

"Just let me do this my way, okay?"

Hal's face fell. "I'm trying to give us an edge. Paige needs it."

"I know." She touched his shoulder. "Come to bed. We both need to be at our best tomorrow."

She led him back to the bedroom, feeling a little guilty for shooting down his idea. Nothing he was suggesting was technically illegal—lawyers paid jury consultants to do all kinds of questionable research—but tomorrow would be hard enough without risking Judge Booker's anger.

They arrived early the next day. Soft morning light slanted through the high windows, and the courtroom held an air of quiet serenity she knew would be replaced by tension soon enough.

She and Hal guided Paige to the defense table. Ever since Donovan had announced that the Commonwealth was seeking the death penalty, Paige had seemed fragile, on the verge of shattering. Today was no different—her hands trembled. Dark circles shadowed her eyes.

Kristina settled into her seat and made a few last-minute annotations to her jury notes. Even without looking up, she could feel Donovan's smirk from across the aisle. It made her grip tighten around her pen.

"All rise," the bailiff's voice rang out. Kristina stood, pushing her shoulders back.

Judge Solomon Booker cut an imposing figure as he strode into the courtroom. His salt-and-pepper hair was neatly trimmed, contrasting with his deep brown skin. His dark eyes scanned the room with quiet intensity.

"Be seated," the judge said. "We're here for jury selection in the case of the Commonwealth versus Paige Hess. Let's begin."

As the first group of potential jurors filed into the courtroom, Kristina studied their faces—not that there was much she could glean just by looking at them. No one appeared happy to be here. They had been pulled unwillingly from their daily routines to participate in a process most of them were barely familiar with, and twelve of them would have their lives further disrupted by being impaneled on the jury.

Judge Booker gave the jurors a moment to settle in before addressing them. "Good morning," he began. "We are here today to determine who will serve as impartial jurors in the trial of Ms. Hess. Your job is simple, but critical—answer all questions honestly. We're not looking for any particular answers, just the truth. This helps ensure Ms. Hess receives a fair trial. Any questions before we begin?"

There were no questions, just weary stares and one yawn.

"Okay, let's get going. Ms. Nolan?"

Kristina stood, smoothing her skirt. She addressed the first prospective juror, starting with easy questions before getting to the substance. "Have you or a close family member worked in law enforcement?"

"My brother was a police officer for thirty years," the man said. "He retired last year."

"And in your opinion, are most police officers trustworthy?"

The man hesitated. "I'm not sure what you mean."

Kristina offered a polite smile. "Well, based on your personal experience, do you feel you could evaluate the testimony of a police officer without giving it more or less weight than other witnesses?"

"I mean, I'll try."

"Thank you for your honesty," Kristina said. She turned to Judge Booker. "Your Honor, I move to strike this juror for cause."

"Any objections, Mr. Donovan?" Judge Booker asked.

Donovan stood. "Yes, Your Honor. The juror stated he would try to be impartial. I believe he should be given that chance."

Judge Booker considered for a moment. "I agree. Ms. Nolan, you'll need to use a peremptory strike if you want to remove this juror."

Kristina flipped through her notes, buying time. The *voir dire* process was as much art as science. Each side had a limited number of peremptory strikes, allowing them to dismiss jurors without cause. The challenge was using these strikes wisely and not wasting them. She studied the juror's face, his body language, one last time.

She hated to burn a peremptory strike on the very first prospective juror. On the other hand, the man's brother had been a cop for thirty years, and Paige's trial involved the alleged murder of a cop. The potential for bias was too great to risk.

"Yes, the defense will exercise a peremptory strike to remove this juror, Your Honor."

As the man left, Donovan threw her a surreptitious wink, knowing she was down one strike. Kristina ignored him.

The questioning continued through most of the day, with Kristina and Donovan taking turns questioning the jurors. As the day wore on, both attorneys used their peremptory strikes strategically, Donovan removing a social worker and other potential jurors who might sympathize with Paige, Kristina striking an Army ranger and other law-and-order types. By the late afternoon, Kristina had used all of her peremptory strikes. Donovan had one remaining.

Kristina's gaze settled on a middle-aged woman in the second row of the jury box. Ruth Baird. Kristina's pulse quickened as she reluctantly recalled the list Hal had created the night before. Baird had been charged with a DUI five years ago.

Kristina stole a glance at Donovan. He leaned against the prosecution table, his posture relaxed.

He didn't know—yet. But if he asked his usual questions, he would elicit the information.

She glanced quickly at Hal. His slight nod was almost imperceptible. She needed to head off Donovan's question. And with Booker presiding, she needed to tread very carefully if she was going to pull that off.

"Ms. Baird," Kristina began, trying to ignore the knot forming in her stomach. "You're a real estate agent, is that correct?"

"Yes, that's right." Baird's voice carried a hint of pride. "I've been with Vance Realty for about twelve years now."

"Any police officers in your family, or other law enforcement members?"

"No."

Kristina paused to make sure she phrased her next question perfectly, and when she spoke, she made her voice sound as casual as possible, barely interested—just another routine inquiry near the end of a long day. "Have any of your close relatives been involved in a DUI?"

Kristina held the woman's stare.

A pause, barely noticeable.

"No," Baird said.

Kristina's stomach twisted with the same nagging discomfort she always felt when she pulled this type of stunt. Unlike Hal, who could blithely manipulate the system without a second thought, she couldn't so easily shrug off the feeling that she'd crossed a line. But ultimately her job was to protect Paige Hess to the best of her ability, and that was a commitment she considered sacred.

"Thank you, Ms. Baird. No further questions."

As Kristina sat down, she felt Donovan's eyes on her. She held her breath, but he moved on to the next potential juror without pressing Baird about her own history.

As the final jury was seated—Ruth Baird among them—Kristina surveyed the twelve faces before her. It wasn't a perfect group, but it was one that would give Paige a fighting chance.

17

———

As Donovan stood to deliver the Commonwealth's opening statement, Hal gave Paige a reassuring pat on her arm. He shot Kristina a glance. After weeks of pre-trial maneuvering, it was finally showtime.

As he'd hoped, the trial had become a high-profile media spectacle. The courtroom gallery was packed with reporters. As Donovan strode toward the jury box, they hushed with a tense energy Hal knew would be reflected in news coverage across the state—maybe even the country.

Given the stakes, Donovan's speech was sure to be a master-class in prosecutorial grandstanding. And Hal couldn't wait to bash it apart.

Donovan buttoned his suit jacket. Hal had to admit Slow Draw cut an impressive figure with his tailored suit and perfect hair. But all the polish in the world wouldn't help him once the jury heard Hal's version of the truth.

"Ladies and gentlemen of the jury," Donovan said, "we are here because a dedicated public servant lost his life. Landon Kirk, a decorated detective with the Philadelphia Police Department, a man who had sworn to protect and serve this city, and had done so for many years, was mercilessly killed in the prime of his life. He was struck with brutal force by an SUV—a vehicle weighing two tons. The impact smashed his body and propelled it like a rag doll. He landed on the asphalt—flesh torn, bones broken, hip pulverized—gasping out his last painful breaths as the vehicle that hit him peeled away into the night. And the most disturbing part is that this collision was not some careless accident. It was an intentional act. It was a murder, committed by the defendant in this trial, Paige Hess."

Hal watched the jurors' reactions. Horror, disgust, anger. Hal had to admit it was a strong opener—Donovan knew how to work a jury.

"I am the prosecutor at this trial, representing the Commonwealth of Pennsylvania. The defendant has lawyers of her own —defense attorneys." Donovan gestured at Hal and Kristina in the same way someone might point out a turd on a sidewalk. "I'm sure they will tell you that it is the Commonwealth's burden to prove the defendant's guilt beyond a reasonable doubt. And they're right. That is my burden, and I will more than meet it. The evidence I will present to you over the course of this trial will prove, beyond any reasonable doubt, that the defendant was behind the wheel of the vehicle that struck Landon Kirk, that the impact killed him, that she fled the scene, and that she did all of this with the premeditated intent to kill."

Hal sensed Paige trembling beside him. He placed his hand over hers and squeezed gently. "It's just rhetoric," he whispered. "We'll have our chance, too."

Donovan's voice took on a quieter, almost somber tone. "You will hear from an assistant medical examiner, Dr. Reyes, who performed an autopsy on Landon Kirk's mangled body. Dr. Reyes will tell you that the impact of the SUV was the cause of Landon Kirk's death. You will hear from a police officer, Barrett Moody, who can definitively place the defendant, in her SUV, within minutes and miles of the crime scene. You will hear from an accident reconstructionist—an expert in his field who examined the defendant's SUV—who will testify that the damage to the front of the vehicle was consistent with a collision with a human body. And finally, perhaps most damning, you will hear from Landon Kirk's grieving widow, who will tell you that her husband and the defendant weren't strangers. They were involved with each other. Because this incident was not a coincidence, ladies and gentlemen. It was not an accident. It was cold blooded murder."

No testimony from Avalos? Not calling the lead detective to the stand during a murder trial was an unusual choice. Hal made a mental note.

"By the end of this trial," Donovan said, "if you have listened carefully to the evidence and applied the law as instructed by the judge, you will have no reasonable doubts. You will have no choice but to return the verdict that justice demands—guilty on all counts, including first degree murder. Thank you."

With a final nod to the jury, Donovan returned to his seat.

Hal met the Cowboy's gaze as he stood from the defense table. Donovan had opened strong, but he and Kristina had faced worse and come out on top.

He approached the jury box, making eye contact with each member, lingering an extra moment on Ruth Baird—she of the DUI record.

Then, leaning on the rail of the jury box, he said, "Wow. Mr. Donovan painted a vivid picture, didn't he? Like something out of a horror movie. And like most horror movies, Mr. Donovan's story was simple, gratuitously gory, and with an easily identifiable villain. Also like a movie, it's fiction."

"Objection!" Donovan half-rose from his chair. "The trial's barely started and Mr. Nolan is already resorting to *ad hominem* attacks, calling me a liar!"

Hal turned to the judge. "I didn't say he was a liar, Your Honor. There are any number of reasons that Mr. Donovan could have gotten his story wrong. Laziness, stupidity...."

Judge Booker slammed his gavel. "Enough, Mr. Nolan. Stick to the facts of the case. Keep Mr. Donovan out of it."

Hal nodded. "Thank you, Your Honor." Returning his attention to the jury, he said, "The truth of what happened here is far more complicated than a horror movie. And far more disturbing."

He paced slowly in front of the jury box. "Over the course of this trial, we will show you that Paige Hess is not the villain of this story. In fact, she's barely a side character. She didn't intend to kill Landon Kirk. She didn't kill him at all. It wasn't her vehicle that hit him. She is, in reality, almost as much a victim here as Kirk. She's the victim of a deliberate frame-up by an underboss of the Philadelphia mob, compounded by police and prosecutorial incompetence."

Hal could almost feel Donovan bristling now, always a positive sign.

"Evidence?" Hal said. "How about the fact that Detective Landon Kirk was killed outside a bar where a known, violent criminal, Diego Messina, was present at the time of the incident?"

A ripple of whispers swept through the courtroom at the mention of Messina's name. Hal pressed on.

"Who's the more likely murderer of this decorated detective —a five-foot-four teacher or a mafioso under investigation by the Philadelphia Police Department? Kind of makes you wonder, doesn't it? Or at least ... *doubt?*"

He let that magic word hang in the air for a moment.

"And what about all this evidence Mr. Donovan bragged about? Doctor this, expert that." Hal shook his head. "Those very experts will have no choice but to admit to you that the so-called evidence is far from conclusive—as will our own expert witness. No one can say for sure that Ms. Hess's Ford Explorer hit Landon Kirk. No one can even tell you for sure that *any* Ford Explorer hit Landon Kirk. These are guesses, not evidence."

Hal turned to meet Paige's gaze, letting the jury see the connection between them.

"No, by the end of this trial, you will be left with far more than reasonable doubt. You will be faced with the chilling reality of our so-called justice system, in which innocent people are accused of crimes they did not commit, while real killers remain free."

Hal straightened. "All we ask is that you keep an open mind. Do that, and I'm sure you'll reach the right verdict. Not guilty. Thank you."

Kristina leaned in close as he sat down, her breath warm against his ear. "Was it really necessary to call Donovan stupid?"

"It was."

"Judge Booker—"

"I thought you did great," Paige whispered. Her hands were still shaking, but there was hope in her voice. "Ariana was right about you."

Kristina gave Hal a long look before turning back to her notes, shoulders tight.

The judge called for a brief recess. In an hour, Donovan would call his first witness, and the real work would begin.

18

————

Hal scanned the faces of the jurors as they returned to the courtroom after the recess, watching for tells. A hard glare, a set jaw, a frown of sympathy—any hint of which way they were leaning after the opening statements. He couldn't get a read.

Kristina's hand brushed his arm and when he turned, she tilted her head toward Paige. Their client sat with her head lowered, her hands clasped tightly in her lap, her lip quivering.

"Hey," Hal whispered. "Remember what we talked about. The jurors will make assumptions based on your body language. The media, too."

"Try to keep your chin up and your eyes forward," Kristina said. "I know it's hard."

Paige sat up straighter. Some of the fear left her eyes. Hal nodded his approval and gave her shoulder a quick squeeze. "We're going to get you through this, Paige. I promise."

Judge Booker's gaze swept the courtroom. "Are both sides ready to proceed?"

"The Commonwealth is ready, Your Honor," Donovan announced.

Hal faced the judge. "The defense is ready as well."

Booker nodded curtly. "Good. Mr. Donovan, please call the Commonwealth's first witness."

"Thank you, Your Honor. The Commonwealth calls Assistant Medical Examiner Julia Reyes to the stand."

Reyes headed to the witness stand. The woman wore a pristine lab coat, her hair twisted back in a tight bun. Hal had tangled with Reyes on more than one occasion. She was a no-nonsense professional, very hard to rattle on the stand. She also had a compulsive need for order, bordering on full-fledged OCD. Even now, he watched as she arranged her notes carefully in front of her and fussed with the microphone.

"Dr. Reyes," Donovan began, "could you please state your qualifications for the court?"

Reyes spoke in clipped, efficient tones. "I'm an Assistant Medical Examiner, working in the Medical Examiner's Office of the City of Philadelphia Department of Public Health. I conducted the autopsy on Landon Kirk."

Donovan nodded, pacing slightly. "Could you describe your findings for the court?"

Reyes leaned forward. "Mr. Kirk suffered multiple traumatic injuries consistent with a high-speed vehicular impact. There were comminuted fractures of both femurs, a crushed pelvis, and severe blunt force trauma to the torso resulting in multiple rib fractures and internal organ damage. The cause of death was determined to be exsanguination due to the severing of major blood vessels."

Hal noticed his favorite juror, Ruth Baird, wince at the description. Her gaze flicked to Paige with a sympathetic look.

"At this point," Donovan said, "the Commonwealth moves to enter the autopsy photographs into evidence."

Kristina stood. "Objection, Your Honor."

"Approach, counselors." Judge Booker waved them toward the bench.

At sidebar, Kristina kept her voice low but firm. "The photographs are unnecessarily prejudicial, Your Honor. Dr. Reyes has already provided detailed testimony about the injuries. The photos serve no purpose except to inflame the jury's emotions."

"The Commonwealth has a right to present its evidence," Donovan said. "The photos demonstrate the severity of the impact, which goes directly to intent."

"How does the fact that my client's vehicle got smashed say anything about intent—" Hal started, but Kristina's look silenced him.

"Your Honor, under Rule 403, these photos' minimal probative value is substantially outweighed by their prejudicial effect. Dr. Reyes's testimony has already established the injuries and cause of death. The photos are graphic and disturbing and would unfairly prejudice the jury against Ms. Hess."

Judge Booker nodded, Kristina's careful legal analysis hitting his sweet spot. "I agree with Ms. Nolan. The photos are excluded."

Donovan flinched. "Your Honor—"

"That's my ruling, counsel." Booker's tone left no room for argument. "Let's move on."

Hal and Kristina returned to their seats. Donovan returned to the well of the courtroom. "Dr. Reyes, in your expert opinion as a doctor and medical examiner, were Mr. Kirk's injuries consistent with being struck by a mid-size SUV, such as a Ford Explorer?"

"Objection." This time it was Hal who lifted his butt from his chair. "Calls for speculation."

"Not speculation," Donovan said. "Expert opinion."

Judge Booker's eyes narrowed. "Overruled. The witness may answer."

Reyes gave a succinct nod. "Yes, the locations of the primary impact points strongly suggest Mr. Kirk was hit by an SUV or a small truck."

Donovan walked back to his table. "No further questions, Your Honor."

Hal approached the witness stand. "Dr. Reyes, always a pleasure to cross-examine you."

She regarded him cautiously. "Good to see you as well, Mr. Nolan."

"You've given us a very thorough description of Mr. Kirk's injuries. But I'd like to clarify something. You used the term 'consistent' quite a few times, didn't you? As well as the word 'suggests'? Those words are kind of wishy-washy, wouldn't you say?"

"Objection," Donovan said.

"What I'm getting at," Hal said, "is that despite your phenomenal level of expertise, it doesn't sound like you can tell us with any certainty what really happened here."

Reyes's expression remained impassive. "I just told you what happened, Mr. Nolan. Mr. Kirk died from injuries consistent with a vehicular impact, likely by an SUV-sized—"

"Likely. Another wishy-washy word."

"Mr. Nolan." Judge Booker's voice carried a stern note of warning.

"Sorry, Your Honor." Hal kept his gaze on the witness. "Are you testifying here today that Mr. Kirk was hit by my client's Ford Explorer?"

"Obviously not—an autopsy wouldn't reveal the owner of—"

"Are you testifying here today that Mr. Kirk was hit by *any* Ford Explorer?"

Reyes adjusted the microphone again, then lined up the edges of two sheets of paper in front of her, before answering. "No. I cannot identify a specific vehicle based solely on the autopsy findings. However—"

"In fact, Doc, isn't it true that these injuries could have been caused by any number of vehicles?"

"Objection, Your Honor." Donovan no longer sounded as calm. "Asked and answered."

"Overruled," the judge said. "The witness may answer."

Reyes adjusted the microphone again. "The injuries are consistent—" She stopped herself, and Hal allowed a small smile. "I can't specify a particular make or model of vehicle," Reyes finished.

"Thank you, doctor. No further questions."

Hal returned to his seat. Not exactly a knockout blow, but a decent a start at creating some doubt in the jurors' minds, doubt that would begin to pile up.

"Redirect?" the judge asked Donovan. The Cowboy seemed to consider asking Reyes more questions, then shook his head. "The Commonwealth is ready to call its next witness, Officer Barrett Moody."

A young cop with a buzz cut walked to the witness stand. As the kid was sworn in, Hal leaned toward Paige and whispered, "This is the guy who pulled you over?"

She nodded. "It's him."

Hal smiled. Moody's crisp uniform and eager-beaver expression screamed *rookie cop*—and rookie cops didn't tend to do well on the stand.

"Officer Moody," Donovan began, "could you please tell the jury about your encounter with the defendant, Paige Hess, on the night in question?"

"Yes, sir." Moody leaned forward, his voice straining for a confident tone he didn't quite achieve. "At approximately 11:50 PM, I observed a blue Ford Explorer driving erratically on Frankford Avenue. The vehicle was swerving between lanes and traveling at inconsistent speeds. I initiated a traffic stop."

"And what happened when you approached the vehicle?"

"I approached the driver's side and made contact with the driver."

"Is that driver here today, Officer Moody?"

The cop nodded. "Yes. Ms. Hess, the defendant. Right there." He pointed.

Hal felt Paige tense beside him.

"Was there anyone else in the Ford Explorer with Ms. Hess?"

"No. She was alone."

"Did you notice anything when you stopped Ms. Hess's vehicle?"

"Yes, sir. There was visible damage to the front of the SUV. The right headlight was shattered, and there were big dents and scratches all over the hood and front bumper."

"What actions did you take next, Officer Moody?"

"I asked Ms. Hess to step out of the vehicle. I performed a field sobriety test. After observing her performance, I administered a breathalyzer test as well."

"And what was the result of that test?"

"Ms. Hess's blood alcohol content was measured at 0.06%."

"Which is below the legal limit of 0.08% but still indicative of alcohol in her system, correct?"

"Objection," Hal said. "Officer Moody is not qualified to offer an analysis of the breathalyzer results."

Judge Booker nodded. "Sustained. Move on to your next question, Mr. Donovan."

"Tell us what you did next," Donovan said.

Moody shifted in his seat. "Given that Ms. Hess was under the legal limit, I issued a warning for erratic driving and let her go."

"What about the broken headlight?"

Moody looked uneasy. "She had promised to get it fixed, so I issued a warning for that as well, rather than a citation."

"And then what happened after she drove away?"

"Approximately ten minutes later, I received a radio call about a hit-and-run incident involving a pedestrian just a few blocks from where I had stopped Ms. Hess. Given the damage I had observed on her vehicle, I called in about my earlier stop, believing it could be related."

Donovan glanced at the jury, satisfaction clear on his face. "No further questions."

Hal stood. "Officer Moody, you described my client's driving as 'erratic.' Can you be more specific?"

"Well, like I said before, she was swerving between lanes and her speed was inconsistent."

"Inconsistent how? Was she speeding?"

"No, not speeding. Just ... varying her speed."

"I see. And this 'swerving' that you observed.... Did Ms. Hess cross into oncoming traffic? Endangering other drivers?"

Moody squirmed. "No, she was just ... not maintaining her lane perfectly."

"So you stopped her because she was not a perfect driver?"

"Objection," Donovan said. "Mischaracterizing the witness's testimony."

"Withdrawn," Hal said with a wave of his hand. "Officer Moody, you also mentioned seeing damage to Ms. Hess's vehicle. Did you ask her about it?"

"Yes, I did."

"And what did she say?"

The cop paused, his gaze flying to Donovan. "Well, she said she had hit a deer earlier in the week."

"Oh. And did you have any reason to disbelieve her?"

"No, sir."

"You didn't see any human brains or eyeballs or anything dripping off her bumper?" Hal managed to keep a straight face, although he was pretty sure he heard a stifled laugh behind him, either from the gallery or the jury box. As for Moody, his face had blanched white.

"No, sir. I didn't see any ... brains or eyeballs."

"How about blood?"

"No, sir. I didn't see any blood."

"Thank you, Officer. No further questions."

As Hal returned to his seat, he glanced at Paige and offered her a reassuring smile. She returned it weakly.

"Your Honor," Donovan said, "the Commonwealth requests a moment to set up some audiovisual equipment. Our next witness is an expert in accident reconstruction, and we intend to use visual aids." His gaze swung to Hal, as if daring him to make another objection.

Hal lounged in his chair, watching Donovan's minions wheel in a projector cart. As far as he was concerned, Donovan's expert could use all the visual aids he wanted. The more elaborate the testimony, the sweeter it would be when Desmond Cobb demolished it.

19

HAL SUPPRESSED an eye roll as Donovan and his DA's Office flunkies fumbled with a projector and screen in the well of the courtroom. Hal had sparred with Slow Draw enough times to know this demonstration would be more sideshow than substance.

"The Commonwealth calls Edward Huffman to the stand," Donovan announced.

A middle-aged man with salt-and-pepper hair and wire-rimmed glasses made his way to the witness stand. He moved with the rehearsed precision of a B-list actor playing a scientist. A professional prosecution witness if Hal had ever seen one.

Hal leaned toward Kristina's ear. "Ten bucks says this guy has a German accent."

A smirk dimpled her cheek. "You're on."

After Huffman was sworn in, Donovan began his questioning. "Mr. Huffman, could you please state your occupation for the Court?"

"Certainly," Huffman replied. "I am an accident reconstructionist." His voice carried the most precise and fastidious accent Germany could produce. Hal held back a smug grin.

"And could you explain to the Court what exactly an accident reconstructionist does?"

Huffman nodded, cleaning his wire-rimmed glasses with the practiced ease of a seasoned showman handling a prop. He replaced them with exaggerated care, pausing for effect before launching into a well-rehearsed spiel.

"An accident reconstructionist investigates and analyzes motor vehicle accidents to determine how and why they occurred. We use a combination of engineering principles, physical evidence from the crash scene, and data from vehicles and other sources to reconstruct the events leading up to, during, and following a collision. Our goal is to provide a clear and scientifically-based explanation of the accident dynamics, contributing factors, and potential causes."

Donovan nodded, clearly pleased with his witness's erudition. "And what are your qualifications in this field, Mr. Huffman?"

"I have a Bachelor's degree in Mechanical Engineering and a Master's in Forensic Engineering. I've been working as an accident reconstructionist for over twenty years, and I'm certified by the Accreditation Commission for Traffic Accident Reconstruction."

Kristina bumped Hal's shoulder. "Does Desmond have that certification?" she whispered.

"Desmond can hold his own against this pompous clown any day."

"I hope so."

In front of the witness stand, Donovan said, "Thank you, Mr. Huffman. Now, in this case, did you examine the Ford Explorer belonging to the defendant at this trial, Paige Hess?"

"Yes," Huffman said. "I conducted a thorough examination of Ms. Hess's Ford Explorer approximately forty-eight hours after the incident."

"And what did your examination reveal?"

Huffman leaned forward slightly, his head turning toward the screen with a dramatic flair. He raised a hand and pointed a small remote at the projector. The device whirred to life.

"Let's dim the lights, please," Donovan said.

One of his lackeys obliged and the room darkened, focusing everyone's attention on the image of Paige's damaged SUV. Its front end was the mess of crumpled metal and shattered plastic Hal remembered from the impound lot.

"As you can see in these images," Huffman said, clicking through more garish photos, "the vehicle showed significant damage to the front end. The right headlight was shattered, and there were dents and gouges along the hood and front bumper."

Hal reached past Kristina to place a reassuring hand on Paige's arm. Paige gave him an almost imperceptible nod, but her jaw was clenched tight.

Of course the jurors were ogling the photos and hanging on every German-accented word.

"In your expert opinion, Mr. Huffman, was this damage caused by the vehicle striking a person?"

"Objection," Hal said, rising to his feet. "Leading the witness."

Judge Booker's eyes narrowed. "Overruled. The witness may answer based on his expertise."

Huffman cleared his throat. "Yes, the damage is consistent with a collision involving a human being."

"Mr. Huffman, can you elaborate on what specific aspects of the damage indicate a collision with a person?"

"First, the height of the primary impact zone is consistent with striking an adult at mid-thigh to hip level." Huffman gestured at the screen. "Additionally, the pattern of dents and scrapes suggests a body being thrown onto the hood upon impact."

"Based on your analysis, can you estimate the speed of the vehicle at the time of impact?"

"I estimate the vehicle was traveling between thirty to thirty-five miles per hour at the point of impact, and likely accelerating."

"Accelerating. So the driver—Ms. Hess—was actually *speeding up* as she rammed the victim?"

"Objection," Hal said.

"Let the witness speak for himself, Mr. Donovan," Judge Booker warned.

"Of course, Your Honor." Donovan nodded, satisfied. "And what would be the likely outcome for a pedestrian struck at that speed, Mr. Huffman?"

"I am not a medical doctor. But based on my knowledge of physics ... it would not be good."

"Thank you. I have no further questions."

Paige leaned toward Hal and Kristina, her voice barely a whisper. "This is bad, isn't it? The jury believes him." Her eyes seemed to plead for reassurance.

"Not when I'm done."

As Donovan returned to his seat, Hal stood. He approached the witness stand with measured steps—Huffman wasn't the only good actor in the room.

Donovan's assistant reached for the light switch, but Hal stopped him with a raised hand. "Leave it. I have some questions about this little slide show."

The assistant froze mid-reach. Donovan gave him a nod, and he left the courtroom dark.

"Mr. Huffman," Hal began, his tone conversational, "you've given us one interpretation of these pictures, but I'd like to explore some other possibilities."

Huffman nodded cautiously. "Of course."

"You mentioned that the damage was 'consistent' with a

collision involving a human being. That's a word we keep hearing over and over again in this trial. *Consistent.* Basically what that means is that it's possible, right? It means maybe?"

Huffman shifted slightly. "It means that based upon—"

"Yes or no please. It's a simple question."

"Yes."

"In fact, in your twenty years of experience, you've seen all sorts of vehicle damage, and sometimes the causes are unexpected. Is that fair to say?"

"Yes, that's fair," Huffman admitted.

"So, let's consider some unexpected possibilities here. Could this damage have been caused by a collision with a large animal—say, a deer?"

Huffman took off his glasses, fiddled with the narrow arms. "Well, the pattern from a deer would typically be different—"

"Yes or no, Mr. Huffman." Hal gestured at the screen. "Could a deer have caused that?"

"Yes."

"What about a runaway shopping cart? I've gotten so many dings from those because people can't return their carts to the corrals like civilized—"

"Objection," Donovan interrupted. "Relevance?"

Judge Booker leaned forward. "Mr. Nolan, where are you going with this?"

"Your Honor, I'm simply exploring alternative explanations for the damage to Ms. Hess's vehicle. Mr. Donovan is presenting one theory out of many, and pretending it's definitive evidence. The jury deserves a little more honesty, don't you think?"

"Objection!" Donovan glared at him. "Another *ad hominem* attack!"

Hal waved a hand. "Oh, don't be so sensitive."

Booker slammed his gavel. "Proceed with your questions, Mr. Nolan. Carefully."

Hal turned back to Huffman. "So, Mr. Huffman, a shopping cart collision. Possible?"

"Highly unlikely given the—"

"Yes or no, please."

Huffman sighed. "It's ... possible, though—"

"And what about a collision with another vehicle? Say, a motorcycle? Possible? Yes or no."

"Yes," Huffman admitted reluctantly.

"During your examination of the vehicle, did you find any blood?" Hal already knew the answer to this, and wanted to make sure the jury knew it, too.

"No."

"No blood?" Hal acted surprised. "So, to summarize, while you *believe* the damage is *consistent* with striking a person, there are other possible explanations, including a shopping cart, a motorcycle, and a deer. Is that a fair statement?"

Huffman paused, his gaze flicking to Donovan.

Hal stepped forward, blocking the witness's view of the prosecutor. "Mr. Huffman, I asked you a question. Does that, or does that not, reflect the testimony you just provided, under oath, to the jury?"

Huffman gave a small nod. "It does."

"Thank you, Mr. Huffman. No further questions."

Donovan stood immediately for redirect. "Mr. Huffman, does the absence of blood on Ms. Hess's vehicle mean that she did not hit Mr. Kirk?"

"No, it does not mean that at all."

"Can you please elaborate, since defense counsel clearly thinks otherwise?"

"It is common for there to be no blood on a vehicle after collision with a pedestrian. This type of impact is more likely to cause internal than external bleeding."

"Objection," Hal said. "I don't recall hearing about Mr. Huffman's medical degree."

"Sustained," Judge Booker said. "Please keep the questions within your witnesses's sphere of expertise, Mr. Donovan."

The Cowboy gave a reluctant nod. "Are there other reasons blood would not be found on the vehicle?"

"Yes. Even if the bleeding is external, clothing may absorb the blood. Also, the impact—especially when the vehicle accelerates into the accident, as I believe occurred here—often throws the pedestrian *away* from the vehicle, further reducing the likelihood of blood transfer."

"Thank you, Mr. Huffman."

As Donovan returned to his seat, Hal felt a bead of sweat trickle down his back. He'd done a decent job of shaking up Donovan's expert, but had it been enough, especially in light of Donovan's redirect? A lot would depend on Desmond Cobb selling their own version—that Paige could have hit a deer days earlier in a completely unrelated accident and the evidence would look the same.

Donovan rose again. "The Commonwealth calls Melanie Kirk to the stand."

20

Landon Kirk's widow, a woman in her late thirties dressed in somber black, made her way to the witness stand. Her face was a mask of grief, and Hal watched as she dabbed her eyes with a tissue. Several jurors' expressions softened.

After she was sworn in, Donovan approached. "Mrs. Kirk, I know this is difficult, but could you please tell the Court about your relationship with the victim in this case, Landon Kirk?"

"He was my husband."

"I'm so sorry, Mrs. Kirk. And how long were you married?"

"It would have been twelve years this December." Her voice broke, eyes glistening.

Donovan paused, giving her time to recover and giving the jury plenty of time to bask in her grief. Finally, in a gentle voice, he said, "What did Landon do for a living?"

"He was a detective with the Philadelphia Police Department."

"A homicide detective, correct? Protecting the city from killers?"

Hal considered an objection based on relevance or leading the witness, but Kirk's position as a homicide cop was one of the pillars of the defense theory, providing a motive for Diego Messina to have wanted Kirk dead. So he remained in his seat and let the testimony play out uninterrupted. There might be cause for objection later, but now was not the time.

"Mrs. Kirk, was your husband investigating a man named Diego Messina at the time of his death?"

Melanie wiped her eyes before looking directly at the jury. "Landon was *not* investigating Diego Messina. No."

And, now was the time. Hal popped up from his chair. "Objection, Your Honor."

"On what basis?" Donovan sneered.

"Oh, I don't know. Lack of foundation? Hearsay? Calls for speculation? Take your pick."

Judge Booker held up a hand. "Settle down, Mr. Nolan. I'm going to allow the question. But don't stray too far with this, Mr. Donovan."

Hal winced, but sat back down.

"Your husband was not investigating Diego Messina." Donovan let the statement hang in the air. "Mrs. Kirk, in the months leading up to your husband's death, did you notice anything unusual about his behavior?"

"Yes. He became distant. He started working late a lot—or so he claimed."

"Claimed?" Donovan said. "Did you have any suspicions about his behavior?"

"Objection," Hal said, half-heartedly. "Leading the witness."

"Overruled."

"Yes, I was suspicious. I thought he might be having an affair."

"An extra-marital affair, you mean?"

Melanie looked down. "Yes."

"What did you do?"

"I watched him. Followed him." She glanced quickly at the jury. "I needed to know."

"And did you discover anything?"

Melanie's eyes flicked to Paige, then back to Donovan. "Yes. About a month before ... before he died, I saw Landon with *her*. With Paige Hess. Having coffee together at a café near the police station."

"Did you confront your husband about what you saw?"

"No. I was planning to, but...." Melanie took a shaky breath. "Before I could work up the courage, she killed him."

"Objection, Your Honor!" Hal said.

"Sustained. The jury will please disregard the last comment."

Donovan smiled tightly. "No further questions, Your Honor."

A murmur rippled through the courtroom. From the corner of his eye, Hal saw that Paige's face had gone pale white. Kristina squeezed her arm gently.

As Donovan returned to his seat, Hal stood. Cross-examining the widow of a murder victim was a task no defense attorney enjoyed. It was all risk, no reward. If anything he said came off as an attack—one mean-spirited word, one tone-deaf question—he risked losing the jury permanently. The best he could hope for was to delicately call a few of her assumptions into question.

"Mrs. Kirk, I am very sorry for your loss," he began. "I know this must be incredibly difficult for you. I just have a few questions to clarify some points, if that's alright?"

Melanie nodded stiffly.

"You stated that your husband was not investigating Diego Messina. How do you know?"

"He would have told me."

"But you testified that you were surprised to see your

husband with Ms. Hess at a café. So clearly, your husband didn't tell you everything."

Melanie shifted in her seat. "Work was different. He shared everything about the job."

The definitiveness of her response dismayed him, but he moved on. "At the café, were your husband and Paige Hess engaged in romantic behavior?"

Melanie hesitated. "I ... I didn't stay long. I just saw them talking."

Hal nodded sympathetically. "And as you testified, you never confronted your husband about what you saw?"

"No," Melanie admitted. "I ... I was afraid of what he might say."

"So you don't know for sure that anything untoward was happening. It's possible that there could have been an innocent explanation, isn't that right?"

Melanie looked down at her hands. "I suppose."

Hal pressed on gently. "Mrs. Kirk, isn't it correct that your husband gave safety presentations at local schools as part of his job?"

Melanie looked up, surprise flickering across her face. "I wasn't aware that Landon did that."

"You—no?" Hal missed a beat, surprised by her answer. "You didn't know he gave active-shooter training?"

"Asked and answered," Donovan objected. Hal caught a note of concern in the prosecutor's voice.

Hal nodded calmly, but internally, his mind kicked into overdrive. Melanie not knowing about the school presentations was the kind of curveball that could turn a trial, but only if the lawyer was confident enough to go off-script to capitalize on it. Thankfully, a lack of confidence had never been a problem for Hal.

"Mrs. Kirk, you testified a moment ago that your husband

was not investigating Diego Messina at the time of his death. You sounded pretty definitive about it."

"That's right."

"In fact, you testified that your husband shared everything about the job."

"I wasn't talking about presentations at a school. I was talking about an investigation. Landon would have mentioned that to me—"

"Are you sure? What's the difference? He didn't mention the school safety presentations. Isn't it possible he didn't mention his investigation of Diego Messina?"

"Objection," Donovan said. "The question assumes facts not in evidence. Mr. Nolan has provided no evidence of any investigation—it's all smoke and mirrors, Your Honor."

"Smoke and mirrors?" Hal scoffed. "Mr. Donovan was the one who raised the issue on direct. He's the one who asked the witness about a Diego Messina investigation. That means I have the right to ask about it on cross."

Donovan knew he was right, and deflated even before Judge Booker overruled his objection.

"Please answer the question, Mrs. Kirk."

Melanie met Hal's gaze. "I guess it's possible there could have been an investigation that Landon didn't tell me about."

"Thank you, Mrs. Kirk. Again, I know this is difficult. I appreciate your honesty."

Melanie nodded miserably.

Hal paused for a moment, then shifted back to his prepared questions. "Mrs. Kirk, are you aware that Ms. Hess is a teacher?"

"I … no. I don't know anything about her."

"I see. Well, she's a teacher at one of the schools where your husband gave safety presentations. Don't you agree that it's possible that your husband and Ms. Hess could have had a professional relationship, something related to these presentations?"

Melanie's gaze moved to Paige, and something changed in her expression—something Hal could only describe as hope, or relief. "Is that what happened? He wasn't cheating on me?"

"Do you think that's possible?" Hal said.

"Objection!" Donovan said.

"I withdraw the question," Hal said. "Thank you, Mrs. Kirk. No further questions."

As Hal returned to the defense table, Donovan rose from his chair on shaky legs. "Redirect, Your Honor?"

"Go ahead."

Donovan approached his witness. "Whether or not your husband was cheating on you, one fact remains. You saw Landon Kirk and Paige Hess together, prior to his death. They were sitting at a café. They knew each other. They were not strangers. Is that a correct statement of your testimony, Mrs. Kirk?"

"Yes, that's correct."

Donovan shot a glance at the jury. "Thank you."

Judge Booker leaned back in his chair. "This seems like a good time to break for lunch. We will reconvene in ninety min—"

The judge's words died as heads turned toward the back of the courtroom. Someone had thrown open the heavy doors with enough force to make them bang against the walls.

21

———

Detective Mateo Avalos burst through the courtroom doors and made a beeline for Donovan. Ignoring the disapproving glares from the deputy sheriffs, he leaned over the railing to whisper urgently in Donovan's ear.

Hal felt his muscles tense. He strained to hear their hushed conversation, but only caught fragments over the courtroom's noise. Whatever Avalos was telling him, the change in Donovan's demeanor was pronounced. The prosecutor's eyes widened and a slow smile spread across his face.

Avalos's face turned and his gaze met Hal's with a nasty grin. *Not a good sign.*

Judge Booker observed the exchange with bemused patience. "Mr. Donovan," he said eventually, "is there something you'd like to share with the Court?"

Avalos backed away from the railing as Donovan stood up. The prosecutor glanced quickly at the jury before returning his attention to the judge. "Your Honor, I think it would be best if we approached the bench."

Booker waved him forward. "Defense counsel, too."

Hal's stomach tightened. He gave Paige's hand a squeeze. "Sit tight. Whatever this is, we'll handle it."

He and Kristina met Donovan at the judge's podium. Booker pressed a button and a hiss of white noise filled the air, keeping their discussion from the ears of the jury. "Well?"

Donovan cleared his throat. "Your Honor, there's been a new development. The Commonwealth has an additional witness we'd like to call."

"A surprise witness?" Hal said. "Come on, Slow Draw, this is desperate even for you—"

"It's not a trick," Donovan shot back. "Your Honor, Detective Avalos has just learned new facts highly relevant to this case. I understand the timing isn't ideal, but—"

"*Not ideal?*" Hal said.

Kristina touched his arm, a signal to shut his mouth. "Your Honor," she said, "allowing the Commonwealth to introduce a new witness at this stage of the proceedings would be a violation of our client's Sixth Amendment rights. It would also violate the Pennsylvania Rules of Criminal Procedure, which mandate timely disclosure of evidence."

Donovan's face reddened. "Your Honor, I haven't had time to research the law on this, but with all due respect to Ms. Nolan, I'm sure there are exceptions to those rules."

Judge Booker glared at Donovan, his patience visibly evaporating. "I'll excuse your lack of preparation for the moment, Mr. Donovan. Tell me who this witness is and your justification for introducing them so late?"

"The witness's name is Dean Everett. He's an Internal Affairs detective with the PPD. We've just learned that Landon Kirk was the subject of an internal investigation at the time of his death. Apparently, he was taking bribes."

Hal couldn't believe his ears. "Why didn't you lead with that, Slow Draw? The victim was a dirty cop?" He turned to the judge with barely-concealed excitement. "Your Honor, the defense withdraws its objection—"

A sharp elbow to his ribs cut him off mid-word. Kristina gave him a meaningful look before her gaze shifted to Donovan. "There's more, isn't there?"

Judge Booker's gaze sharpened. "Let's hear it, Donovan. All of it."

Donovan's grin returned. "The Internal Affairs investigation revealed that one of the people making payments to Detective Kirk was the defendant, Paige Hess."

Hal tried to keep his expression steady for Donovan's benefit, but even his years of courtroom experience couldn't stop the color from draining from his face. He glanced at Kristina, catching a fleeting glimpse of panic in her eyes, then glanced behind him at the defense table, where Paige Hess sat looking at her hands.

No more secrets. She'd promised him.

"Detective Everett is here in the courthouse right now," Donovan said, "ready to testify to all of this."

"Your Honor, this is completely unacceptable," Kristina said. "We move for an immediate mistrial."

Donovan laughed. "A mistrial, Kristina? You wish!"

Kristina's stare was venomous. "*Wyatt* has clearly been withholding crucial evidence."

"That's not true, Your Honor. We only just received this information ourselves. The Commonwealth has acted in good faith throughout trial."

"You call this good faith?" Kristina said.

Hal couldn't resist jumping into the fray. "Your Honor, an Internal Affairs investigation doesn't materialize overnight. Slow Draw here had a duty to disclose any ongoing investigations related to the victim. He held this evidence back to ambush us."

Judge Booker held up a hand, silencing the three of them.

"Mr. Donovan, when exactly did you become aware of this Internal Affairs investigation?"

"This morning, Your Honor. I immediately instructed Detective Avalos to get more information. He received the details about Ms. Hess's involvement moments ago and came straight here."

Hal pounced on the admission. "Your Honor, even if we accept that explanation, the prosecution still failed to disclose potentially exculpatory evidence this morning. That alone is grounds for a mistrial."

"I wanted to confirm that the evidence was accurate."

Judge Booker leaned back, his expression thoughtful. "I'm not prepared to declare a mistrial at this point. But I am deeply concerned about the timing of this revelation, Mr. Donovan."

Kristina leaned forward. "Your Honor, at the very least, the defense needs time to investigate these new developments. We can't be expected to cross-examine a surprise witness without proper preparation. We request at least a week to properly—"

"Two days," Judge Booker cut her off. "I know it's not a lot of time, Ms. Nolan, but I can't afford to give you more than that. We'll recess until Thursday morning." He fixed Donovan with a stern glare. "And Mr. Donovan, I expect full disclosure of all evidence related to this Internal Affairs investigation to be delivered to the defense's offices by personal messenger—at the DA's expense—within the hour. Use your own credit card if necessary."

Donovan nodded. "Yes, Your Honor."

The judge turned off the white-noise and announced an early end to the day. As the jurors began to to file out of the jury box and the lawyers stepped back from the bench, Hal's gaze landed on their client.

Paige's eyes widened as Hal stalked toward her. Kristina caught his arm. "Not here."

Some of the jurors had turned curious gazes toward them, as had reporters in the gallery.

"Let's get her back to the office," Kristina whispered.

"Okay," Hal said. "But then she's all mine."

22

———

HAL STRODE out of the courthouse with Kristina, the two of them flanking Paige on either side. The bright afternoon sun was blinding. When his vision adjusted, he saw a crowd of reporters surging toward them.

"Ms. Hess, did you deliberately target Detective Kirk?"

"Mr. Nolan! What's your response to the prosecutor seeking the death penalty?"

"Can you address the relationship between Ms. Hess and the victim?"

"Any comment on the Commonwealth's accident reconstruction evidence?"

"No comment," Hal barked, his tone sharper than he intended.

Kristina shot him a look. "No comment?"

"I can't do this right now."

Several of the reporters looked as surprised as Kristina. The Nolan Law Firm—and Hal in particular—was not known for shying away from publicity.

"I think we should say a few words to the press," Kristina murmured close to his ear.

Hal knew she was right. Media attention for the firm had been his justification for taking Paige's case *pro bono*. And aside from the free publicity, public sympathy could sway the jury. But the shock of Donovan's revelation—and the realization that Paige was still withholding critical information from them—had knocked him off balance. He couldn't face the reporters' hungry expressions.

"You talk to them," he told Kristina. "I'll get the car."

She peered at him for a moment, but didn't argue. "Okay."

The reporters pressed closer, microphones thrust forward. Hal spotted a group of deputy sheriffs loitering nearby, looking more interested in the spectacle than in maintaining order. He shouldered his way over to them. "Can one of you help get me through this circus?"

The deputies exchanged glances. One of them, a heavyset man, said, "I can get you to the parking lot."

"Perfect."

The reporters hushed as Kristina began to answer their questions. With the deputy's help, Hal cut through the crowd. He usually thrived on scenes like this, but right now, the press of bodies seemed suffocating. By the time they reached the relative quiet of the parking lot, his shirt was sticking to his back.

"I'll take it from here," Hal said. "Thanks for your help."

"You're defending that woman who killed a cop, aren't you?"

"She didn't do it." Hal unlocked the Toyota. "Or at least, that's what she says."

The deputy snorted. "But they all lie, don't they?"

Apparently. Hal opened the door, slid into his car. "Look, I can't talk about it, okay? Attorney-client privilege."

"I don't know how you live with yourself—"

Hal slammed the car door closed, cutting off the deputy's speech. "Me, either."

Judge Booker had granted them two days. No time at all.

Why the hell would Paige Hess have been paying money to Landon Kirk?

The deputy tapped the window and gave Hal the finger, then turned and trudged away. *Nice.*

He forced himself to breathe slowly, to center himself. That's when he heard a slight rustle of movement from the back seat.

Before he could react, cold metal pressed against the base of his skull. Hal's blood turned to ice, his breath catching in his throat.

"Didn't think you'd need a reminder," a gravelly voice said from behind him.

Hal's eyes found the masked face in his rearview mirror. It was the same man from the alley—apparently, he'd escalated from knives to guns. Hal's hands gripped the steering wheel, knuckles white, fingernails digging into his palms. The world narrowed to a pinpoint, until he was aware of nothing except the pressure of the gun's barrel against the back of his head. Terror clawed at his insides, threatening to overwhelm him.

"Please put the gun away," Hal managed to choke out.

"What's the matter, lawyer?" The gun pressed harder, digging painfully into the base of his skull. "Gun-shy?"

A cold sweat broke out across Hal's skin.

"Don't like repeating myself," the masked man said. "Lose the trial—"

Hal slammed his palm against the horn. The sudden blare cut off the man's threat. Hal felt the weight of the gun lift as the man snarled a curse.

Hal kept his hand on the horn.

For a split second, his eyes locked with those of the man in the rearview, and Hal saw cold fury. Then the rear door opened and the masked man bolted.

Hal slumped forward, forehead resting on the steering

wheel. Bile rose in his throat. He barely succeeded in keeping it there.

It took several long minutes before he could straighten up, before his hands stopped shaking and he could breathe.

His phone vibrated, making him jump so hard the top of his head brushed the Camry's ceiling. It was Kristina. "Are you coming?" she said. "I've run out of soundbites and these reporters are relentless."

"On my way." With trembling fingers, he started the car.

23

———

THE NOLANS' office felt tiny with five people crammed around the conference table. Hal sat at the head, Kristina to his right, Lena to his left. Across from him, Paige hunched in her seat, looking small and defeated, her fingers working at a loose thread on her sleeve. Beside her, Ariana sat perfectly still. The only sound was the faint whine of the building's old pipes, a high-pitched reminder of the state of their law practice and their case.

When Hal finally broke the silence, his voice was low, barely under his control. "Is it true? You were paying Kirk?"

Paige's gaze remained fixed on her hands. "I had no choice."

"Do you want to die, Paige? Because that's where this is heading. They're going to strap you to a chair and administer a lethal injection."

Kristina placed a calming hand on his arm. "Hal...."

He ignored her, unable to look away from his client. "*Why didn't you tell us?*"

Paige jumped, then took a shaky breath. "I'm sorry. I thought—"

"Really? Are you sure? Because thinking doesn't seem to be your strong-suit!"

"Hal!" This time he turned, and Kristina gave him a look that shut his mouth. The room fell quiet, and Kristina said to Paige, "If we're going to help you, we need to understand exactly what happened. We only have a few days to prepare for this new witness."

Tears streamed from Paige's eyes. She leaned into her sister, who wrapped an arm around her shoulders and stroked her matted hair. "I ... don't even know where to start."

"Just start talking," Lena said.

Paige nodded, shuddered. "There was this parent, Mr. Delvecchio. He'd been sending me angry emails—complaining about his daughter's grades, accusing me of favoritism. I've dealt with situations like that before—every teacher does—but Delvecchio was different. I'd heard rumors about him. He was divorced and people said he'd ... hurt his wife. And supposedly he had connections—scary ones from North Philly. One day, he came to my classroom after hours while I was alone grading papers. He was drunk. Belligerent. He started yelling at me. I was scared."

"You never told me about this," Ariana said.

"Don't interrupt her," Lena said. "Please."

Paige's eyes gleamed with tears. "He started screaming, calling me names, getting in my face. I ... pushed him. He stumbled and fell, hit his head on a desk. I don't think it was serious, but I don't know. He said he was going to go to the police. Press charges against me."

"And that's where Kirk came in?" Lena said.

Paige nodded. "He was the only cop I knew. He told me not to worry—that he would handle it. I don't know what he did, but Delvecchio didn't press charges. He didn't do anything. He never contacted me again."

"But that wasn't the end of it, was it?" Kristina said softly.

"No," Paige whispered. "A week later, Landon showed up at my ... my apartment. He said he'd done me a favor, and now I owed him. He wanted money. If I didn't pay, he'd investigate my 'assault' on Mr. Delvecchio—including talking to the administrators at my school. I would have lost everything."

Hal shot to his feet. "Paige, do you have any idea how bad this looks?"

"How much did Kirk demand?" Lena pressed gently.

"Five thousand. I thought if I just paid him, he would be satisfied. But he kept coming back, demanding more."

"How much more?"

Paige stared at her hands. "I've paid him sixty-thousand, maybe sixty-five."

"Jesus, Paige!" Ariana's composure cracked.

Hal slammed his palm against the wall, ignoring the pain that vibrated up his arm. "Well, the prosecution has a clear motive now—the final element of their case. They'll paint you as a desperate woman, willing to kill to end the blackmail and keep your secret."

"But I didn't do it!"

Hal would have laughed at her naïveté if he weren't so infuriated. "Maybe we could have proved that if you hadn't cut our legs out from under us."

"Back off, Hal!" Ariana's voice had an edge, reminding him of other times they'd argued, back when they were different people. "Can't you see how upset she is?"

"She should be upset, Ariana."

"She's the victim here. The jury will see that."

"The jury will see what Donovan wants them to see—a killer." He took a deep breath, trying to rein in his frustration.

"What if we put Paige on the stand?" Lena said. "Let her explain to the jury."

Kristina was already shaking her head. "We can't do that. Putting Paige on the stand exposes her to cross-examination. It gives Donovan a chance to twist her words. One moment of hesitation, one poorly chosen word, and we could easily be in a much worse position than we are now."

"Worse?" Hal snorted. "Not sure that's possible."

Ariana rose from her chair and crossed the room to stand at Hal's side. "Hal, stop. You're brilliant. You'll figure this out."

"Brilliant?" Hal shook his head, acutely aware of how close she was standing.

"Yes, brilliant." She touched his arm, the scent of her perfume stirring dormant memories. He stepped back, catching Kristina's slight shift in her chair.

"Let's just focus on next steps." He returned to his chair, leaving Ariana standing alone. "We need a strategy to deal with this, and we need it fast."

Kristina stared at him for a moment, her lips pressed into a thin line. "Maybe there's a legal basis to exclude the Internal Affairs detective from testifying," she said at last.

"Didn't Judge Booker already shoot that down?"

"He ruled against a mistrial. We can still file a motion *in limine* to exclude evidence. Argue that the prejudicial effect would outweigh the probative value."

Paige looked up. "You mean there's a chance they won't hear about the payments?"

Hal mulled over the idea. "But if we keep the IA detective off the stand, that means the jury won't hear about Kirk being dirty, either. We lose the part of the evidence that could help us."

"It's worth it to exclude the evidence that Paige was paying off Kirk," Kristina argued. "Like you said, that's a motive."

Hal nodded. "Okay. Let's give it a shot. We don't have much time."

"I'll draft the brief tonight and we can get in front of the judge tomorrow for a hearing."

24

———————

THE NEXT MORNING, Kristina walked with Hal down the hallway toward Judge Booker's courtroom.

"I can't believe you researched, drafted, and filed the brief in one night," Hal said, shaking his head.

"And yet you're one who's *brilliant*." Her fingers curled into fists at the memory of Ariana touching Hal's arm the day before. She had to force her fingers to relax.

Hal glanced at her as they walked. "She has an inflated opinion of me, that's all."

"No, *you* have an inflated opinion of you. *She's* just using that to seduce you."

"She's not doing that—"

"She is, Hal. Lena agrees with me. She saw it, too."

Before Hal could respond, they pushed through the heavy doors and into the courtroom. The gallery and jury box were empty. Judge Booker had closed the courtroom for this evidentiary hearing, which meant there was no jury to impress, no reporters to play to—only the lawyers, the judge, and pure intellectual combat.

This was her arena, where *she* was brilliant. Let Ariana try to compete with her here.

"We'll talk about this later," Hal whispered.

Donovan was already at the judge's bench. His eyes lit up at their approach. "You two look happy."

"Don't even start," Kristina warned.

Judge Booker looked at them and sighed. "It's too early in the morning for this."

"I agree, Your Honor," Donovan said. "This motion *in limine* is nothing but another Nolan stunt. They're playing for time because they aren't satisfied with the two days the Court provided them." He fixed his gaze on Kristina. "There's no trick too low for them."

Kristina could feel Hal's agitation beside her, knew his head had just filled with ten vicious comebacks to put Donovan in his place, and that holding them back physically pained him. But he managed to keep his silence.

"Your Honor, with all due respect, my motion speaks for itself," she said.

Donovan interrupted with a derisive snort. "Hardly."

"Enough of that." Booker leveled a stare at Donovan. "The Court intends to hear the defense's motion, Mr. Donovan, so I suggest you save your performance for the jury and prepare some actual legal arguments."

Donovan shifted his weight, his shoulders stiffening. Kristina took a deep breath, steadying herself as Judge Booker's gaze returned to her.

"I read your brief, Ms. Nolan," he said. "You argue the Internal Affairs investigation and these payments are both irrelevant and unfairly prejudicial. However, the fact that your client was making payments to Detective Kirk strikes me as highly relevant—it suggests a motive to kill him."

"Your Honor, we respectfully disagree. The Internal Affairs

investigation was incomplete at the time Detective Kirk died. No conclusive determination was made. The investigation could have ended with his complete exoneration. Yet, Mr. Donovan seeks to present Detective Kirk's corruption as a fact."

"And the payments from your client to Kirk?"

"Those are even more problematic. The payments are dollar amounts with no context. That's not evidence, Your Honor. It's innuendo."

"This is ridiculous," Donovan cut in. "The jury has a right to hear about all of this."

Kristina ignored him. "Furthermore, even if the Court finds some tenuous relevance, this evidence would create an inference of guilt and unfairly prejudice the jury against Ms. Hess."

"An inference of guilt?" Donovan's face flushed. "She was paying him off!"

"Mr. Donovan," Judge Booker admonished, "you'll have your turn soon enough. Continue, Ms. Nolan."

"Your Honor, allowing this evidence would essentially put Ms. Hess on trial for an entirely separate matter—an unproven police misconduct case instead of the charges she actually faces."

Booker sat back in his chair, seeming to consider her arguments. The silence stretched. Finally, he said, "Mr. Donovan?"

"With all due respect, Your Honor, do I really need to respond to this nonsense?"

Booker's eyes narrowed. "You do."

Donovan let out an exasperated breath. "The defense is attempting to hide crucial evidence from the jury. For one thing, the payments establish a clear connection between Ms. Hess and the victim, regardless of context. But even more importantly, there is no conceivable legitimate reason for a teacher to be making payments to a homicide detective. Not willingly, anyway —and that is a clear motive for wanting him dead. The jury needs to see the whole picture, not just the convenient parts the defense wants to show."

Kristina's pulse quickened as she watched Judge Booker study Donovan. "And how do you respond to the defense's argument about unfair prejudice, Mr. Donovan?"

"Your Honor, any evidence that points to guilt could be considered 'prejudicial.' That doesn't make it unfair, or inadmissible."

"Your Honor," Kristina started.

The judge raised a finger. "I've heard enough. Ms. Nolan, while I commend you on a persuasive argument, I'm simply not convinced that these facts are not relevant, or that their prejudicial effect outweighs their probative value. The defense's motion to exclude is therefore denied. I'm allowing the Commonwealth to call Detective Everett."

Kristina's stomach dropped. "Your Honor, I must object—"

"Your objection is noted," Judge Booker cut her off sharply. "And my ruling stands. Now, unless there's anything else, we're going to proceed tomorrow morning with the testimony of Detective Everett."

"Yes, Your Honor."

Judge Booker gathered his files. As soon as he left the courtroom, Donovan turned to Kristina and Hal with a triumphant smile. "Did you work all night doing legal research, Kristina? Those bags under your eyes really bring out the defeat in your face."

Hal stepped between them. "She's twice the lawyer you'll ever be, Slow Draw. Enjoy your hollow victory. It won't change the outcome of the trial."

Donovan's smile widened. "The outcome of this trial is going to be the death of your law firm."

They watched Donovan stroll out of the courtroom. The

smug bastard actually whistled a tune, mercifully cut off when the heavy doors clanged shut behind him.

"Booker made a bad call," Hal said. "It happens. You were fantastic."

Kristina managed a half-smile. She appreciated the support, but they both knew what it was worth. "Sorry I got angry about Ariana. I just—"

"Hey. She's got nothing on you."

"How are we going to be ready for Detective Everett tomorrow?"

"I don't know, but we will be. Because Donovan's right about one thing—we can't afford to lose this one."

Her mind flashed to the countless late nights they'd spent building their firm from scratch, fueled by nothing but determination and an unwavering belief that they could do it. The whispers of doubt from their law school peers, the dismissive looks from established attorneys in the Philly criminal bar—all of that had only added fuel to their fire. It had taken a seemingly endless series of battles to prove that she and Hal deserved their hard-won place in Philadelphia's legal arena.

And there was no way in hell they were surrendering now.

25

———

THE NEXT MORNING, Donovan called Detective Dean Everett to the stand.

A tall, lean man strode to the well of the courtroom. Close-cropped sandy hair, cold blue eyes, the swagger of a cop who'd never doubted himself—Hal disliked him on sight.

As Everett was sworn in, several jurors—both women and men—sat forward in their seats with increased interest. Hal glanced at his client. Despite his anger, Paige's pale face and trembling hands made it hard not to feel sympathy.

Things were about to get ugly.

Donovan began his direct examination, establishing Everett's credentials. Twenty years with the PPD, twelve in Internal Affairs. The detective lounged in his chair as he answered, speaking with easy confidence and tossing occasional smiles at the jury while Donovan led him through his background.

"Detective Everett, can you tell the Court about the investigation you were conducting into Detective Landon Kirk at the time of his death?"

Everett nodded, his expression turning serious. "About seven months ago, we received an anonymous tip suggesting Detective

Kirk was accepting bribes. Based on this tip, we quietly opened an investigation."

"What did this investigation entail, Detective?"

"We monitored Detective Kirk's activities over the course of several months, and tracked his financial records."

"And what did you find?"

"We discovered a pattern of suspicious deposits into Detective Kirk's accounts—both small and large sums of money."

"What conclusion did you draw from that?" Donovan said.

Everett's expression hardened, as if the question pained him. "Our investigation led us to suspect that Detective Kirk was probably engaged in the solicitation and acceptance of unlawful inducements in exchange for official actions."

"Objection, Your Honor," Hal said, rising to his feet.

"On what grounds?" Donovan said.

"Besides abuse of a thesaurus? For one thing, his testimony is pure speculation—"

"Overruled, Mr. Nolan." Judge Booker's hard stare cut him off.

Hal sank back into his chair. He caught Kristina's eye, saw the tightness around her eyes. Paige looked ill.

"By unlawful inducements," Donovan said, "you mean bribes?"

Everett looked at the jury. "We have various terms for it. Unlawful inducement. Extralegal payment. But in layman's terms, yes, I'm referring to bribery."

"The deposits couldn't be explained by a legitimate side business?"

"No."

Hal could see that Donovan and Everett had the jury's rapt attention now. And they'd only just gotten started.

"What did you do after discovering the suspicious deposits?"

"We attempted to trace them," Everett said.

"To their sources, you mean?"

"Correct. We hoped to link the deposits to known criminal elements."

"Were you successful?"

Everett's expression soured. "Partially. The subjects in these cases tend to be sophisticated in their methods of concealing financial transactions. While the larger transfers proved untraceable, we successfully identified the source of several smaller deposits. One originated from a pawn shop previously under investigation for receiving stolen property—an investigation that had mysteriously been terminated. Another traced back to a local pharmacist suspected of illegally trafficking in narcotics."

"Were you able to trace any other transfers, Detective?"

Hal's stomach tightened. By now, everyone in the room knew where this testimony was heading.

"Yes. Our investigation revealed a series of recurring payments from an unexpected source—a high school teacher with no prior criminal history or apparent connection to criminal enterprises."

"That must have surprised you, Detective."

Everett shrugged.

"Is that teacher present in the courtroom today?"

"Yes." Everett pointed at the defense table. "The defendant, Paige Hess. She made payments totaling $62,000 to Landon Kirk's personal account through multiple separate transactions."

A collective gasp went up from both the jury and the gallery. Hal didn't need to look to know that every pair of eyes now stared at Paige. He heard the unmistakable sound of fingers tapping phone screens as the reporters worked frantically to turn this revelation into news.

Judge Booker rapped his gavel. "Order!"

The sharp crack of wood on wood echoed through the courtroom, but it did nothing to silence the rumble of conversations that had broken out across the room.

Donovan waited until the noise subsided before continuing. "Detective Everett, in your professional opinion, what reason would a schoolteacher have for making such substantial payments to a homicide detective?"

"Objection!" Hal was on his feet again. "Calls for speculation."

"Detective Everett is an expert—"

"Then lay the groundwork," Booker said, cutting him off.

"Yes, Your Honor." Donovan nodded, quickly regaining his composure. "Detective, is it fair to say you have a lot of experience with bribery investigations?"

"In my twelve years with Internal Affairs, I've investigated over two hundred cases involving allegations of bribery or other financial misconduct."

"And in your extensive experience, have you ever encountered a situation where payments of this nature from a civilian to a police officer were for legitimate purposes?"

"No, I have not."

Donovan gave the jury a meaningful look, then said, "No further questions."

As Hal rose from his seat, Kristina softly cleared her throat—a warning. They both knew sparring with Everett would be treacherous. The detective was smart, confident, and seasoned on the stand. But if Hal didn't land at least a few good jabs, Paige's case might never recover.

He took a breath as he faced the Internal Affairs detective across the well of the courtroom. "Detective Everett, you testified about an ongoing investigation into Detective Kirk. Was this investigation concluded before his death?"

Everett's eyes narrowed slightly. "No, it was not."

"Were any official, definitive findings made regarding Detective Kirk's alleged misconduct?"

"No."

"The unlawful inducements you mentioned were suspected, but not proven. Correct?"

"The investigation terminated with the subject's death, but had it continued—"

"Thank you, Detective. Now, regarding the payments from Ms. Hess to Detective Kirk. You've told us about the amounts and the frequency. But you cannot tell the Court the specific reason for these payments, can you?"

"As I told Mr. Donovan, in my experience—"

"I'm not asking about your experience. I'm asking about the evidence you discovered during your investigation."

Something flashed behind Everett's cold blue eyes. "No," he said slowly. "The investigation did not uncover a specific reason for the payments."

Hal nodded, turning to face the jury. "Let's be honest. These payments could have been made for any number of reasons. Maybe Detective Kirk did some handiwork for Ms. Hess. Maybe he sold garden gnomes through his Etsy store."

That got a laugh, as he'd hoped. Even Detective Everett flashed a grin. "We didn't find any garden gnomes, Mr. Nolan."

"Did you look?"

"Objection," Donovan called out. "Argumentative."

"I'll move on," Hal said, "What if Ms. Hess felt threatened by the father of one of her students, and Detective Kirk provided personal security services?" He wouldn't put Paige on the stand to testify to that, but nothing stopped him from planting the idea in the jury's mind—*a lawyer trick as old as time.* "That's possible, isn't it?"

"Is that what she claims?" Everett said.

"Sorry, Detective—only *I* get to ask the questions. My point is, aren't all of these innocent explanations for the payments possible?"

"Technically possible, but—"

"Thank you, Detective," Hal said, cutting him off again. "One more question. In your investigation, did you find any evidence —any at all—directly linking these payments to Detective Kirk's murder?"

Everett's jaw tightened. "No, we did not."

Hal returned to his seat.

"Redirect?" Judge Booker said.

Donovan rose from his chair. "No, Your Honor. The Commonwealth rests."

Booker nodded. "We'll take a ninety minute recess for lunch. When we reconvene, the defense may call its first witness."

26

———

LUNCH WAS in a sandwich shop a block from the courthouse, packed with the usual crowd—lawyers and paralegals rushing through their meals, the occasional judge chugging a coffee. Hal stabbed at a wilted salad, his fork scraping against the cheap cardboard bowl. He barely tasted the food. His mind wouldn't stop replaying his cross-examination of Dean Everett, wondering if he could have done more to undermine the Internal Affairs detective.

"Garden gnomes?" Kristina took a sip of her iced tea, her eyes sparkling with amusement. "Where did that come from?"

"It just came to me." Hal pushed a cherry tomato around his bowl. "I thought it was a pretty good line."

"It was." Kristina leaned forward, put her hand on his sleeve. "Hal, you did as much as you could."

"I know."

In the chair next to Kristina, Paige pushed her own salad around, untouched. "What happens now?"

"The Commonwealth rested its case," Kristina said. "That means from this point on, *we* control the trial."

"And the trial is going to be all about Diego Messina," Hal added. "We'll put a few Foul Line regulars on the stand, as hostile witnesses if we have to. They'll put Messina at the scene. Then we hit the jury with Messina's arrest records—the violent ones. By the time we're done, the jurors will barely remember Donovan's witnesses. They'll be so convinced Messina was behind Kirk's death, half of them won't even remember *you're* the one on trial."

Paige looked doubtful. "How do you know Messina's guilty?"

He threatened to kill me, for one thing. But Hal decided not to mention his visits from the masked man or his encounter with Messina in the stairwell of Paige's apartment building. Instead, he picked at his salad.

"It isn't our job to know who's guilty. We're not trying to convict anyone. All we're doing is suggesting to the jury that there's at least one plausible alternative to the prosecution's story. That gives us reasonable doubt, and that's all we need."

"Eat some of that salad," Kristina said. "It's going to be a long afternoon."

They left the sandwich shop, stepping into the midday sunshine to head back to the trial. As they drew closer to the courthouse, Hal stopped short. A crowd had gathered, bristling with cameras and microphones.

"Damn." Hal grabbed Kristina's arm and started to steer her and Paige in a different direction.

Kristina gave him a questioning look. "What's with you lately? You love the press."

"Not today."

"You already dodged them once. We *need* the media on our side, and no one is better at talking to them than you."

He took a deep breath, knowing she was right. "Fine."

As they approached, microphones thrust toward them from

all sides. Questions overlapped, demanding comments about the Internal Affairs testimony.

Hal offered a practiced smile. "As we've stated from the beginning, Ms. Hess is innocent. The truth will come out very soon."

"But what about the payments to the victim?" A microphone jabbed toward his face. "Can you explain them?"

"We look forward to examining all of the Commonwealth's so-called evidence in court. The DA's case is not nearly as solid as they'd like you to believe."

"How do you respond to speculation that your history with Aldo Burke is driving the prosecution's aggressive stance?"

Hal couldn't hold back a smirk. "You'd have to ask that question to Aldo Burke. We're focused on demonstrating our client's innocence."

The more he talked, the more this started to feel like old times. He was almost enjoying himself when a blonde reporter pushed into his path. "Mr. Nolan, given the high-profile nature of this case, are you concerned about a repeat of the Hazenberg incident?"

The world compressed to a pinpoint. Hal opened his mouth to respond, but no words came out. Memories flooded his mind —the deafening crack of a gunshot, blood, searing pain.

He felt Kristina's hand on his back, gently pushing him toward the courthouse doors. "We're due back in court," she told the blonde. "We'll answer more questions later. Thank you."

In the lobby's sudden quiet, Hal let out a shaky breath. Kristina's eyes searched his face, full of concern.

"I'm fine," he said. "Just ... brought back some memories."

"Memories of Hazenberg?" she said. "Or of a man in a mask? Hal, maybe I was wrong. Maybe we should have called the police."

Paige looked from one of them to the other. "What man in a mask?"

"No, you were right," Hal said. "We can use the threats as additional evidence that Messina's behind this. Sending a thug to try to manipulate the trial? It will catch Donovan totally off-guard."

They headed for the elevator. Hal jabbed at their floor and the elevator car lurched into motion.

"And what if he makes good on his threat?" Kristina said. "Hal, he's already come at us with a knife and a gun."

As Hal watched the numbers rise, something tugged at his memory.

"A knife and a gun?" Paige's voice shook.

Then it came to him. "*Gun-shy.*"

"What?" Kristina stared at him.

"At the shooting range, when I met with Donovan and Avalos after Paige's arrest, Avalos asked if I was still 'gun-shy.'"

Kristina's face tightened. "Avalos is an asshole."

"Agreed, but that's not my point. The masked man used those exact words when he put a gun to my head. What if it isn't Messina who's been threatening us? What if it's Avalos?"

"Hal, think about what you're saying." Kristina shook her head. "We *know* whose been threatening us. Diego threatened you at Paige's apartment and he wasn't wearing a mask."

"Exactly. Why threaten us anonymously if you're also going to show your face? Makes no sense."

"And you think it makes more sense that a homicide detective would tamper with a murder trial?"

"Avalos's anger issues aren't exactly a secret. And he's desperate for a win. Plus, he hates me."

"Can someone please explain what's happening?" Paige's voice cracked.

Their phones buzzed simultaneously. They shared an apprehensive look before reaching for them.

Hal read the message, then looked up to find his shock mirrored in Kristina's eyes.

Diego Messina was dead.

27

———

INSTEAD OF RETURNING to the courtroom, they spent the afternoon in separate interrogation rooms at Police Headquarters. Hal had not seen Kristina in hours.

The milieu was typical police bullshit. A chair so uncomfortable it inflicted muscle cramps. A rancid level of body odor most homeless people failed to achieve. Harsh lighting that cast shadows across Avalos's face, making the detective look even more pissed off than usual.

Hal yawned deliberately.

"You enjoying yourself, Nolan? Because I can do this all day."

"A mindlessly repetitive task? Of that I have no doubt."

Avalos loomed over him, muscles bunching beneath his leather jacket. His dark eyes boring into Hal's. Hal had spent the last hour needling him with every snide comment he could think of, noting the camera in the corner and hoping it was wired for sound so his buddies could rib him later.

"One more time," Avalos said, each word precise with suppressed rage, "this time without the wisecracks."

"No promises."

"Where were you today between 11 AM and 12 PM?"

"As I've already told you multiple times, Kristina and I were at lunch with our client at a crowded sandwich shop. You can corroborate it—there were plenty of witnesses. In fact, I'm sure you already have."

Avalos said nothing.

"You can also look at the footage recorded five minutes later by the legion of reporters interviewing us outside the court-house," Hal said.

Avalos glared at him.

"Or maybe your theory is that between the salads and the interviews, we slipped away to slit Diego Messina's throat."

"Not all murders are committed firsthand," Avalos said, his hand curling into a fist.

"So you're saying what? We hired a hit man?"

"How about your investigator, Lena Randall? She was a Marine, right? Trained to use a combat knife? Where was she?"

Hal's laugh echoed off the concrete walls. "You think we sent Lena to murder Diego Messina? Why the hell would we do that?"

"I'm exploring all possibilities." Avalos leaned forward. "That's what good police work is all about."

Hal snorted. "Good police work is not a subject you're quali-fied to speak on. You're the worst detective—"

Avalos surged forward, his face nearly touching Hal's. "Doesn't it seem convenient? Messina being murdered moments before you're about to make him out to be a killer at Hess's trial? Now he can't deny your ridiculous story."

Hal's anger flared. "How can I spell this out for you in small words you'll understand? Messina's death doesn't benefit Paige's defense. It benefits the prosecution. I'm surprised you're here at all. I would have thought you and Slow Draw would be celebrating down on the ranch, you seem so hellbent on winning this trial at any cost."

Avalos's eyes narrowed. "If you're suggesting that I'm taking this case personally, then you're right. Paige Hess killed a cop, Nolan, and you know it."

"What I know," Hal said, "is that she's innocent until proven guilty. And you haven't proven anything."

"Let's talk about these threats you supposedly received. The one in the alley and the one in your car."

Hal's jaw clenched. "Kristina told you about them?"

"At least one of you has the brains not to withhold critical information from the police."

And also the brains not to tell him about the encounter with Messina in Paige's building.

"Those threats aren't relevant," Hal said.

"No? It wasn't Messina threatening you?"

"That's not his style."

"Maybe you decided the best way to protect yourself was to have Lena Randall take him out."

"That's *definitely* not Lena's style."

"You tell the jury you're going to show them Diego Messina is the real killer. Then you get threatened by a masked man telling you to lose the trial. Then Diego Messina mysteriously gets his throat slashed."

Hal leaned back in his chair. "You really want to talk about the masked man? Fine. Let's talk about him. He cared an awful lot about Paige's trial. Almost like he was taking it personally." Avalos stiffened, his expression darkening. "But you know what's really interesting? How the masked man seemed to know when the trial wasn't going the prosecution's way. How he knew exactly when and where to find us. How he knew my fear of guns. Own any masks, Detective?"

Avalos slammed both hands on the table. "You son of a bitch."

Hal didn't flinch. "I'm just exploring possibilities. Isn't that what good police work is all about?"

Avalos wheeled away from him, his face filled with disgust. "I can't stand you, Nolan. Everything people say about you is true. You don't care about justice. You don't care about truth. All you care about is winning, no matter who gets hurt."

"You're projecting," Hal said. "It's a psychology term. You should look it up."

They glared at each other. Finally, Avalos muttered a long string of curses and left the room.

Hal slumped in his chair. Other than muffled sounds from beyond the thick door, the silence in the room was complete.

More hours crawled by as Avalos let him stew—another standard cop ploy. He forced himself to focus on Paige's trial, the only thing that really mattered right now. Messina's death muddled things. Juries preferred a living, breathing villain, not a dead one. But Hal believed he could still use Messina's presence at Foul Line to create reasonable doubt. And he still had Desmond Cobb, their accident expert, to hammer home Paige's claim that the damage had been caused by a deer. They were still in the game. Could still win.

The door swung open. Avalos entered, this time with Kristina. Hal felt a wave of relief seeing her.

"Your alibis checked out," Avalos announced.

"You don't say."

"You're free to go."

Hal stood, stretched his stiff limbs, and joined Kristina in the doorway.

"What about Lena?" she said.

The detective's expression hardened. "Ms. Randall is still in custody. Unlike you two, she doesn't have an alibi for the time of Messina's death."

"I want to talk to her," Kristina said.

Avalos shook his head. "I don't think so. She's a person of interest in an ongoing investigation."

"We're her attorneys," Kristina said. There was an undercurrent of steel in her voice—it didn't surprise Hal, but it did impress him. "So you will let us see her. Right now."

28

───────

AVALOS GRUDGINGLY SHEPHERDED them across the homicide bullpen. Kristina matched his pace. As far as she was concerned, the detective had already abused his authority by keeping her and Hal here on the flimsiest of bases—there was no way she was going to allow him to further detain her cousin without probable cause.

Avalos stopped in front of an interrogation room indistinguishable from the ones that had held her and Hal. She assumed Hal must have made the detective miserable for the past several hours, because she could feel the rage radiating from him. He paused by the door, glowering at her.

Her instinct was to take a step back—put space between them—but she didn't. Avalos was like an angry dog, growling, tensed for attack. If she showed any hesitation, he'd go for her throat.

She felt Hal shift closer, ready to intervene, but this was her fight. She held Avalos's stare.

"All right, counselor." Avalos reached for the door handle. "Let's do this."

"Hold on. You're going to wait out here. And you're going to turn off all recording devices. This is a privileged conversation."

Around them, the usually hectic bullpen fell silent. She could feel dozens of cops watching them.

Probably taking bets on whether we walk out of here alive.

Avalos's nostrils flared. "Okay. When you talk to her, maybe you can explain that withholding information from the police is a bad idea."

"All I'm going to tell her is that we're leaving."

She gave him a final glare, then wrapped her fingers around the door handle. As soon as she and Hal were inside, she closed the door firmly behind her, relieved to put a barrier between her and Avalos.

Any relief she felt was short-lived. The air in the interrogation room was so cold it raised goosebumps on her arms. An ancient-looking vent rattled overhead, and she had no doubt Avalos had turned up the AC intentionally.

"The old deep-freeze," Hal muttered. "Classic PPD."

Kristina shivered. The room was small, oppressive. Bare walls, a metal table, four metal chairs. Lena sat ramrod straight in one of them, her fingers splayed on the table's surface.

Her eyes snapped to them, sharp and alert as ever. But there was fear there, too.

"Everything's going to be okay." Kristina slid into the chair across from her cousin and took her hand. Lena's skin was like ice, and the chair was so cold against Kristina's thighs she half-worried her skin would fuse to the metal.

Hal started to drape his suit jacket over her shoulders, but she shrugged it off. "Give it to Lena. She's been in here for who knows how long."

Lena took the jacket gratefully, pulled it around herself. "Thanks, Hal."

Kristina caught the subtle shift in Lena's expression—a softening that anyone else would have missed. Just months ago, her cousin would have refused any gesture from Hal, distrusting him to his core. This small moment—accepting his jacket in a cold interrogation room—might seem minor, but to Kristina it was a sign that maybe Lena had finally started to see the man she'd married.

"They're saying I'm a suspect in Messina's murder," Lena said in a tone of disbelief.

"A person of interest," Kristina corrected. "They don't have enough evidence to call you a suspect."

"It's a calculated maneuver by Donovan and Avalos," Hal said. Kristina could sense him pacing behind her. "Take away our resources, throw us off balance just as it's time to present our defense."

"But it won't work," Kristina said. "We're going to get you out of here." She leaned forward. "Based on the questions Avalos is asking, it sounds like Messina was killed with a knife sometime between 11 and 12:30 today. I need you to tell us exactly where you were."

"At the office. Doing research for the case."

"What time did you get there? Did anyone see you?"

"About 10 AM. I didn't notice anyone."

"You're sure? No one was outside? Maybe a panhandler? Anyone?"

Lena shook her head. Her look of misery made Kristina's heart clench. "I don't think so."

"Let me think." Kristina chewed her lip. "Did you make any calls? Texts?"

Lena shook her head again. "I was deep into research for the case. I didn't even look up until the cops starting banging on the door. By then it was later, closer to 1."

"What kind of research were you doing?" Kristina said. "Anything online? Did you log into any databases?"

Lena seemed to think about the question. "I did some digging around on Philly Beat—it's a forum where Philadelphia cops post about the job."

"You have an account, even though you're not a cop?"

Lena nodded. "You don't need to be a cop. I created one when I finished my tour and was considering a job with the PPD." Lena's gaze flicked nervously to Hal. "I know you're thinking I should have used a fake name, but I didn't want to be there under false pretenses."

"This is the one time," Hal said, lifting a finger, "probably the *only* time, I'm going to agree with your rule-following behavior."

Kristina nodded along with him, feeling a surge of relief. If Lena had logged in to the forum with her personal identity and password, there would be a digital timestamp. Maybe not the strongest alibi, but an alibi Avalos would have to consider—especially with no other evidence connecting her to the crime.

"This is good, Lena. We can work with this."

Kristina stood from her chair and turned to the door, but Hal said, "Kristina, wait a second."

She looked at him, then at her cousin.

"Lena," Hal said, "what were you looking for on that forum?"

Lena's eyes lit up, and she seemed to temporarily forget her problems. "I was seeing if I could find anything posted by Landon Kirk—anything that might provide us with more information about what he was up to when he died."

"Well don't hold back now," Hal said. "I can tell by that grin that you found something."

"Kirk was gunning for a promotion. His lieutenant is retiring in a few months. Kirk put in for the job."

Kristina didn't see the significance. "How does that relate to Paige's case?"

"It might not," Lena said. "But I thought it was interesting that he was competing against another detective for the job. Detective Mateo Avalos."

"Hold on." Kristina exchanged a quick glance with Hal. "Kirk and Avalos were rivals for the same promotion?"

"I guess Avalos will get it now," Lena said.

"Which means Avalos," Hal said, "had a motive for wanting Kirk dead. And a motive for wanting Paige to take the fall."

Kristina tried her best to avoid her husband's infuriating, knowing grin. "You're jumping to conclusions."

"So what if I am?" Hal resumed his pacing, his energy palpable. "With Messina dead, we need another shady figure to point the finger at. Who better than Avalos? A cop with a motive and a temper. This must be why Donovan didn't put Avalos on the stand."

"We don't know that," Kristina said.

"And the best part is Avalos *probably did it*. If he's bold enough to threaten us, attack us—"

"No, Hal. You *want* Avalos to have done it. That doesn't mean he did. We don't know that Avalos had anything to do with any of this—Kirk's death or the threats against us—you just hate him."

"No. *He* hates *me*. And he might as well have handed me his card when he called me gun-shy. It wasn't a coincidence."

Kristina felt herself losing ground. "Think about the jury. We'd be asking them to believe that Avalos murdered a fellow detective and framed an innocent woman—for what? A job promotion?" She took a deep breath, gathering her thoughts. "Diego Messina is much more plausible. Blaming him is still our strongest play, even if he's dead."

"I disagree," Hal said.

Kristina saw Lena pull the jacket more tightly around her shoulders and felt a pang of guilt. "We can argue about this later. Right now, we need to get Lena out of here."

29

―――――

KRISTINA EXITED THE INTERROGATION ROOM, Hal close behind. She tuned out the chaos of the homicide bullpen, her focus zeroing in on Detective Avalos. He leaned against a desk, arms crossed, a smirk playing at the corners of his mouth.

"Let me do the talking," she said under her breath.

"I can't wait," Hal said.

As she strode toward Avalos, she caught sight of another figure approaching from the opposite direction. Wyatt Donovan. Apparently while she and Hal had been talking to Lena, Avalos had called for legal backup.

He's going to need it.

Avalos straightened, his expression hardening. "Done speaking with your *client*, Ms. Nolan?"

"You're going to release Ms. Randall right now."

Avalos shook his head. "She's not going anywhere. I already told you she's a person of interest in an ongoing investigation."

Donovan reached them, taking up a position next to Avalos. "Is there a problem here?"

Kristina kept her voice low and controlled. "The *problem* is that your detective's continued detainment of Ms. Randall without formal charges is a violation of her Fifth Amendment rights. You're both treading dangerously close to a Section 1983 action."

Donovan flinched, but recovered quickly. "Spare us the civil rights lecture, Kristina. Detective Avalos has every right to question a potential suspect."

"Potential suspect? Based on what evidence?"

Avalos jumped in. "She doesn't have an alibi for the time of Messina's murder."

"Do you?" Hal said.

Kristina shot Hal a warning glance before turning back to Avalos. "Ms. Randall was at our office, working on the Paige Hess case."

"Prove it," Avalos said.

"Gladly. She logged into an online forum."

She saw a flicker of uncertainty cross Avalos's face, but Donovan stepped in. "What's that worth? For all we know, Ms. Randall could have logged in and then left the office."

Their confrontation had drawn attention, the bullpen falling silent for the second time and a lot of angry cops looking their way. Kristina could sense Hal's back straightening and hoped he'd keep quiet.

She lowered her voice. She kept her gaze on Donovan, hoping he would be more rational than Avalos. "Think about this, Wyatt. Detaining Ms. Randall isn't just a violation of her rights, it's bordering on a Brady violation. By preventing our investigator from working on the case, you're effectively suppressing potentially exculpatory evidence. Judge Booker rejected our first motion for a mistrial, but maybe he'll take another look after he hears about this interference with our defense preparation."

She saw Donovan's face go a shade paler and pressed her advantage before he could respond. "Release Ms. Randall now, and we can pretend this lapse in judgment never happened. But if you continue to hold her, I'll be in Judge Booker's chambers within the hour. And I'll be filing an ethics complaint with the State Bar as well."

"*You'll* file an ethics complaint?" Avalos laughed, but it sounded forced.

"Try me."

The silence stretched as the four of them stared each other down. Donovan's jaw worked. She could sense him calculating the risks. Finally, he turned to the detective. "Let her go." Avalos opened his mouth, but Donovan raised a hand, cutting off his protest. "*Now*, Mateo."

Avalos stormed away to collect Lena from the interrogation room.

"Smart move," Hal said to Donovan. "I guess you are capable of making those from time to time."

"You better hope there's no evidence tying you to Messina's death," Donovan said. He lowered his voice. "Avalos would love a chance to hang you."

"Why is that, do you think?"

They were interrupted when the detective arrived with Lena, who was still wearing Hal's suit jacket. Kristina took her cousin's arm. "Let's get out of here."

Outside the police station, Kristina took a deep breath of the cool night air, feeling the tension in her shoulders ease slightly.

"How did you get me out of there so fast?" Lena said.

Hal laughed with a shake of his head. "Let's just say Slow Draw will probably cry himself to sleep tonight—after he researches Section 1983 actions."

"What are those?"

Hal shrugged. "No idea."

Kristina nudged Hal with her elbow, allowing herself a small smile. The victory felt good, but it was tempered with the knowledge that Donovan would be out for blood tomorrow. She squared her shoulders. "Let's go home."

30

Day one of the defense's case began the next morning. Hal started things off with two regulars from Foul Line, a couple of middle-aged men with beer bellies who reluctantly placed Diego Messina at the sports bar on the night Landon Kirk was killed.

But their testimony sounded more like a eulogy, every "was" and "used to be" reminding the jury that Messina was dead, beyond questioning. Hal sensed the jurors shifting uncomfortably as he tried to pin a murder on a man who couldn't defend himself. His instincts screamed at him that he was forcing the trial in the wrong direction—going against the jury's subconscious requirement for fair play.

And the real killer was right there in the gallery. Every time he glanced at the spectators, he caught Avalos's cold stare.

He was relieved when the time came to call Desmond Cobb to the stand—the insurance appraiser-turned-expert witness. At least his testimony wouldn't lead them down a dead end.

In his ill-fitting suit and comb-over, Desmond looked like a nerdy accountant as he made his way to the witness stand.

The ultimate wolf in sheep's clothing.

Desmond had barely finished being sworn in when Donovan leapt to his feet. Hal wasn't surprised. After suffering Kristina's verbal takedown the night before, the prosecutor had to be itching for payback. As expected, he immediately launched into an objection.

"Your Honor, I object to this witness being qualified as an expert. Mr. Cobb is a former insurance appraiser, not a forensic specialist."

Hal smiled pleasantly at Judge Booker. "Actually, Mr. Cobb's expertise as an insurance appraiser is directly on-point, Your Honor. As an insurance appraiser, Mr. Cobb has many years of real-world, in-the-field experience assessing vehicle damage and determining repair costs. He's developed an extensive knowledge of accident reconstruction."

Judge Booker's gaze swung back to Donovan. "Do you have a response to that, Mr. Donovan?"

Donovan's jaw pulsed. "Your Honor, this is a murder case, not a fender-bender. The Commonwealth maintains that Mr. Cobb's expertise is not sufficient for the complex analysis required."

"Overruled. I'll allow Mr. Cobb's testimony. The jury can decide how much weight to give his expert opinion."

Hal nodded to the judge, then approached the witness stand. "Mr. Cobb, now that we've established your bona fides, could you please tell the court about your examination of Ms. Hess's vehicle?"

Desmond leaned forward with a serious, almost somber expression—a demeanor that could not be more different than the one he'd displayed at the impound lot while joking about dead cops and llamas. "I examined the Ford Explorer at the police impound lot. Based on my analysis of the damage patterns, I can confidently say that the evidence is inconclusive regarding whether this vehicle struck a person."

In the jury box, Ruth Baird actually let out an audible sigh of relief. Hal smiled inwardly. The woman who'd narrowly avoided a DUI charge was identifying with Paige, almost as if she were the one on trial—just as he'd hoped. Now he had to get the rest of the jurors on Paige's side.

"Could you please elaborate on that for the jury?" Hal said.

"I would be happy to." Desmond offered the jurors a polite smile, which several of them returned. "The damage to the front end of the SUV was consistent with a variety of possible impacts. While it could have been caused by striking a person, it is equally possible that it resulted from hitting a large animal or a low-riding vehicle. Without more definitive evidence, it's impossible to state with certainty what caused the damage."

"So, in your expert opinion, Mr. Cobb, is it possible to conclusively state that Ms. Hess's vehicle was involved in Detective Kirk's death?"

"Objection!" Donovan called out. "Calls for a legal conclusion."

"Overruled," Judge Booker said. "The witness may answer."

Desmond shook his head firmly. "Absolutely not. It is not possible to make that conclusion based solely on the vehicle evidence I examined. If the prosecutor's expert said that, he was not being truthful."

"Objection!"

"Sustained," Judge Booker said. "The jury will please disregard that last comment. And Mr. Cobb, there's no need to attack the Commonwealth's witness."

Desmond gave the judge a contrite look. "I'm sorry, Your Honor. It just upsets me when someone uses their fancy credentials to fool people."

"Objection!"

Hal coughed into his fist, finding it harder not to laugh. "Mr. Cobb, is it possible that the damage to Ms. Hess's SUV was caused by an impact with a deer?"

"Yes, that is entirely possible."

"Thank you, Mr. Cobb. No further questions at this time."

Hal returned to his seat. He knew Kristina well enough to sense she was struggling not to roll her eyes, but he thought he sensed some approval in her expression as well. *And we haven't even reached the main event.*

Donovan was already at the witness stand, in full attack mode. "Mr. Cobb, isn't it true that you were once charged with insurance fraud?"

"Objection, Your Honor," Hal said. "Prejudicial and irrelevant."

"Goes to credibility," Donovan said.

Judge Booker's eyes narrowed. "Overruled. I'd like to hear the answer."

Desmond faced the prosecutor with a bemused expression, and Hal suppressed another smile. If Donovan thought Desmond Cobb would be an easy man to rattle, he was about to experience a very rude awakening.

"Yes, that's correct." Desmond's voice was casual, matter-of-fact. "I was charged with insurance fraud several years ago. It was a false allegation."

"According to you," Donovan said with a sneer.

"According to a jury. I was found not guilty."

"Lucky for you." The sneer fell away, Donovan's jaw twitching. "By the way, who was it that represented you at that trial, Mr. Cobb?"

"The Nolan Law Firm represented me."

Donovan's eyes widened with feigned surprise. "So is it fair to say you owe the Nolans a favor?"

"Objection, Your Honor." Hal spread his hands. "While I am happy to stipulate to my firm's incredible legal skills, I fail to see how they are relevant here."

"Goes to bias!" Donovan snapped.

"I don't owe anyone a favor," Desmond said mildly. "I've been engaged for my expertise on vehicle damage, and that's what I'm providing. Or at least I'd like to, if you would ask me any questions about that."

Donovan's face flushed red. The courtroom filled with murmurs and a few laughs. Judge Booker clapped his gavel, but there was a faint smile even on his face. "Mr. Donovan?"

"No." Donovan shook his head. "No further questions."

As soon as Donovan returned to his seat, Hal rose. Kristina looked at him with surprise, as did Donovan. Everyone had assumed Desmond's testimony was done.

"I have a few questions on redirect, Your Honor," Hal said. The judge gestured for him to proceed. Hal couldn't resist flashing Donovan a grin as he stepped into the courtroom's center.

"Mr. Cobb, what was the basis of the accusation made against you in that insurance fraud case?"

Donovan's head popped up, his expression one of anxious confusion. He had the good sense to suspect a trap, even if he clearly had no idea what it was. "Relevance, Your Honor?"

"You asked my witness about the accusation," Hal said. "I have the right to explore the issue on redirect."

The judge nodded. "Proceed, Mr. Nolan ... if you really want to."

"I do, Your Honor." To Desmond, he said, "You can answer the question, Mr. Cobb."

"I was accused of tampering with a vehicle during my assessment, manipulating the damage to support my appraisal. As you helped prove at my trial, the accusation was false and I was exonerated."

"Is it common for insurance appraisers to face that kind of accusation?"

"It happens."

Hal nodded. "In your years of experience as an insurance appraiser, have you ever encountered cases where vehicles did, in fact, appear to have been tampered with?"

From the corner of his eye, he saw Kristina's face go pale, her head making tiny movements as she tried to warn him off without the jury noticing. But there was no stopping now.

Understanding dawned on Donovan's face as well, the trap finally coming into view. "Objection, Your Honor!"

"On what basis?" Hal said.

"This is beyond the scope of redirect—"

"It is not. You opened the door."

"It's irrelevant and speculative and ... prejudicial."

Hal turned to Judge Booker. "Your Honor, I'm simply exploring all possible explanations for the supposed evidence presented by the Commonwealth's accident reconstructionist."

Judge Booker's eyes narrowed. "Tread carefully, Mr. Nolan."

Hal returned to Desmond, whose eyes were now glittering with mischief. "Yes," he said, "I have encountered cases where vehicles appeared to have been tampered with."

"And in your expert opinion, is it possible that the vehicle in this case—the Ford Explorer—could have been tampered with by the police to implicate Ms. Hess?"

"Objection!" Donovan shouted, his face flushed. "Your Honor, please!"

"Yes," Desmond said over the prosecutor's shouts. "It certainly wouldn't be the first time tampering occurred in the police impound lot."

The judge pounded his gavel, his face livid. "The Commonwealth's objection is sustained! Mr. Nolan, this is not what I consider treading carefully!"

Hal shrugged. Treading carefully had never been his forte. Glancing at the jury, he found what he was looking for—curiosity, engagement, receptivity. A dead mobster had not excited them. A dirty police force did. *Game on.*

"No further questions, Your Honor."

31

———

TO HER CREDIT, Kristina didn't explode until they were in the privacy of an attorney-client conference room down the hall from the courtroom. She waited until the door was closed behind them and Paige had settled into a corner before turning on Hal. He braced himself, watching the storm gather in her eyes.

"What the hell was that?" Her fists clenched.

The space, barely larger than a closet, seemed to shrink around them. Hal backed into the small table that dominated the cramped space. Caught in the crossfire, Paige watched them with the nervous expression of a child about to witness a parental brawl.

"It was the first step in getting Paige out of this mess," he said, wincing at the defensiveness he heard in his own voice.

"It wasn't what we planned—what we agreed on." Kristina's breath caught for a second, her face twisting. "We decided on a strategy together!"

Hal looked away. He hadn't intended to hurt her feelings, but the stakes were high. "The strategy wasn't working. We needed to pivot."

"To Avalos?"

Muffled sounds filtered through the thin wall—voices, hurried footsteps, the ding of an elevator. Hal knew they didn't have much time before trial would resume.

"Yes. Messina's dead. Avalos is alive, sitting in that courtroom." Hal leaned forward. "I think we should call him as our next witness."

Kristina's eyes widened. "You have got to be kidding me. Hal, we spent every cross-examination working up to a theory that Messina killed Kirk—*every single cross-examination*. It's what we promised the jury in our opening statement. We can't just abandon that theory now and point to Avalos instead."

"It's our best move."

"And I suppose your hatred of Avalos is just coincidental?" Kristina crossed her arms.

"We've been over this. *He* hates *me*—" Hal shrugged. "Yes, it's a coincidence. A happy coincidence. But this isn't personal."

"Really? The shooting range? Him calling you gun-shy? Your belief about him being behind the threats—putting a knife to my throat and a gun to your head? Of course it's personal. You want to take him down."

"So what if I do?" Hal's voice hardened.

"Changing strategies mid-trial is too risky."

"Sometimes risks pay off."

"And sometimes they blow up in your face. If we start throwing multiple theories at the jury, we'll lose them. Keep It simple—that's the first rule of trial work."

Hal rolled his eyes. "Don't you ever get tired of all your rules? We're not in law school anymore, Kristina. Rules don't matter. There's only one thing that matters." He raised a finger, practically sticking it in her face. "Reasonable doubt."

Kristina batted his hand away so hard it banged against the wall. They stared at each other.

A small voice from behind him startled them both. "Do I get a vote?"

"No!" They snapped in unison.

"You're wrong on this one," Kristina said. "We need to deliver one straightforward story to the jury."

"Heaven forbid we challenge them to think."

"You're disregarding decades of trial strategy, backed by hundreds of jury studies."

"*Other* juries. Not ours. I've been watching them. They can handle complexity. They *want* it." He ran a hand through his hair.

"I've been watching them, too," Kristina said. "Watching them start to believe our narrative about Messina." She stepped closer to him. "This isn't about their intelligence. It's about clarity. A coherent story is a credible story. Multiple conflicting stories look desperate."

Hal felt his shoulders sag under the relentless weight of her logic. "Maybe that's true. Fine. But I can break Avalos on the stand, Kristina. You know I can."

"Enough!" Paige's voice silenced both of them.

Hal blinked. For the first time, he glimpsed the strict teacher who'd existed before the frightened client.

"Seriously," she said, "is this what I get for hiring a married couple as my lawyers? *My life is on the line.* Work out your personal issues at home." She fixed them both with a stare Hal could easily imagine terrifying a roomful of kids. "Hal, your instincts got us this far. If you think we should call Avalos to the stand, then do it." She turned to Kristina. "And you—there are libraries that can't match your knowledge of the law. Unleash it. Give Hal what he needs to tear this detective apart."

Hal grinned. Kristina rubbed her temples.

"I don't want to die for a crime I didn't commit," Paige said.

"So the two of you better march back into that courtroom, function as a team, and win this trial."

32

BACK IN THE COURTROOM, Kristina had just settled into her chair at the defense table when a sudden movement caught her eye.

Lena strode purposefully to the defense table. Kristina watched as she leaned in close to Hal, pressing a document into his hand.

Please let this be what we need, Kristina thought, watching Hal's face as he scanned the page. His slight grin told her everything.

"Nice work, Lena."

Lena nodded and retreated to the gallery just as Judge Booker arrived and called the court to order. Everyone stood.

"Is the defense ready to call its next witness?" the judge said.

"Yes, Your Honor," Hal said. He paused—never able to resist a dramatic moment. "The defense calls Detective Mateo Avalos to the stand."

The courtroom erupted with whispers and startled gasps. Kristina kept her face impassive as her gaze darted around the room, taking in Judge Booker's raised eyebrows, Donovan's flushed face, and Avalos's wide-eyed surprise. The detective sat stiffly in the gallery, where he'd expected only to be a spectator today.

"Objection, Your Honor!" Donovan said. "We had no warning that Detective Avalos would testify at this trial—"

"He's on the Commonwealth's own witness list," Hal said.

"Yes, but we didn't call him—" Donovan sputtered. "With all due respect, Your Honor, we didn't anticipate that the defense would choose to call our own detective in what is an obvious ploy—"

"Overruled," Judge Booker said. "What you anticipated is not relevant here, Mr. Donovan. Detective Avalos was listed as a potential witness."

The prosecutor's shoulders slumped. "Yes, Your Honor." He cast a glance behind him at the gallery, and Kristina followed his gaze to a man in the back row. Aldo Burke. The head of the DA's Office Homicide Unit looked furious.

Avalos approached the witness stand, glaring at Hal and her as he passed the defense table.

"I hope you know what you're doing," Kristina murmured to Hal.

"Me too," he whispered back, the ghost of a smirk on his face.

His attempt at humor did not reassure her. No matter how cavalier he might pretend to be, they both knew this stunt would need to be handled carefully. Avalos would be worthless to their case unless Hal could provoke him.

And Hal's ability to do that would hinge on convincing Judge Booker to declare Avalos hostile.

Permission to treat Avalos as a hostile witness would give Hal the latitude to ask leading questions, impeach Avalos's honesty, and—to use Paige's words—tear the detective apart. But persuading a by-the-book judge like Booker to do that would be no easy task, even for them.

"Detective Avalos," Hal began, "let's talk about your relationship with Landon Kirk. You two were close, weren't you?"

Avalos shifted in his seat, his expression guarded. "We were colleagues."

"Just colleagues?" Hal's eyebrow arched. "Not friends? Not rivals?"

"Objection," Donovan called out. "Argumentative and leading the witness."

"Sustained," Judge Booker ruled. "This isn't a cross-examination, Mr. Nolan."

Not yet, Kristina thought.

Hal nodded, undeterred. "When you say you were colleagues, do you mean you were both homicide detectives at the Philadelphia Police Department?"

"Leading the witness," Donovan said.

"I'm just asking for a clarification of Detective Avalos's testimony," Hal said.

Judge Booker nodded. "I'll allow it."

"Yes," Avalos said. His eyes narrowed with suspicion. "Landon and I were both detectives in the Homicide Division."

"Detective, were you aware of any promotions coming up in your department around the time of Detective Kirk's death?"

Avalos's jaw tightened. "I don't see how that's relevant."

"That's not really your decision to make, is it?"

"Objection!" Donovan cast a pleading gaze at the judge. "Your Honor, Mr. Nolan persists in asking leading questions. He continues to badger the witness. This is completely inappropriate."

"Your Honor," Hal said, "I asked a simple question. The witness is being evasive."

Judge Booker frowned. "Please answer the question, Detective Avalos."

Avalos glared at Hal. "There are always promotions coming up. It's a big department."

"Any you were interested in yourself?"

Avalos's face flushed with anger. "I know what you're doing, you smug bastard—"

"I'm just asking questions."

"Detective Avalos," Judge Booker warned, "mind your language. And Mr. Nolan, please get to the point."

Hal held up his hands. "My apologies, Your Honor. I'm simply trying to get straightforward answers from the detective. It seems unusually difficult."

"I don't recall being interested in any job openings." Avalos's glare had turned deadly.

"Your Honor, at this time, I request permission to treat Detective Avalos as a hostile witness."

"Objection!" Donovan shouted. "This is outrageous, Your Honor."

"Approach the bench," Judge Booker ordered, his expression stern.

Kristina felt a tingle of anticipation as she followed Hal and Donovan to the judge's bench. Booker flipped the switch to start the white noise.

"Your Honor," Donovan began, "this is a blatant attempt by the defense to cross-examine their own witness. Detective Avalos is not hostile—he's simply frustrated. As, frankly, am I."

Judge Booker turned to Hal. "Mr. Nolan, on what grounds are you claiming hostility?"

Kristina stepped in. *One shot at this. Make it count.* "Your Honor, if I may respond?" At the judge's nod, she continued. "Since taking the stand, Detective Avalos has been consistently evasive, refusing to give direct answers to straightforward questions. His demeanor has been openly adversarial, even going so far as to call Mr. Nolan a smug bastard."

"He *is* a smug bastard," Donovan bit out.

"Yes," Kristina said, "but that's not an appropriate statement from a witness during courtroom proceedings."

Donovan scoffed. "Your Honor—"

"I wasn't finished," Kristina said. "Detective Avalos's unwillingness to cooperate fully will severely impede our ability to present our case effectively, which would violate Ms. Hess's constitutional rights."

Judge Booker's jaw clenched, probably at the thought of her presenting the same arguments to an appeals court.

"The hostile witness designation exists precisely for situations like this," Kristina said, "where a witness's demeanor and reluctance to testify impede the presentation of relevant facts."

"Relevant facts?" Donovan's face had grown so red he looked like he might burst. "Mr. Nolan is asking him about job opportunities!"

Kristina kept her gaze on Booker. "By allowing us to treat Detective Avalos as hostile, the Court would be serving the interests of justice and ensuring the jury has all the facts needed to make an informed decision."

Judge Booker's expression was thoughtful as he seemed to consider. After a moment, he spoke. "Mr. Nolan, you may treat Detective Avalos as a hostile witness." Hal grinned, turning toward the witness stand with an eager gleam in his eyes. "But," the judge added, "I caution you to use this privilege thoughtfully. This is not carte blanche to badger the witness."

"Thank you, Your Honor," Hal said. Leaning toward Kristina, he added in a whisper. "And thank you."

Kristina gave him a subtle wink. "Go get him."

Hal wasted no time. "Detective Avalos, isn't it true that at the time of Detective Kirk's death, both you and Detective Kirk were candidates for a lieutenant position within the Philadelphia Police Department Homicide Division?"

Avalos's teeth flashed. "What are you implying, Nolan?"

"Your Honor," Hal interrupted, "I'd like to enter into evidence as a Defense Exhibit a document from Detective Landon Kirk's personnel file."

Hal handed Avalos the document that Lena had brought in moments earlier—a document Donovan had assumed was buried safely beneath the mountain of discovery materials he'd provided.

"Detective, what does this document show?" Hal's voice carried just enough edge to make several jurors shift forward in their seats.

Avalos's jaw tightened. "It shows Landon's application for the lieutenant position." His gaze darted between the document and Hal like a cornered animal searching for escape.

"A moment ago, you testified that you were not interested in this position, correct?"

"No. I said I didn't recall being interested in any openings."

"Ah. And does this document refresh your recollection?"

"Not really, no." Avalos glared defiance at Hal. "I don't remember being interested in this position."

"Well, let me help you with that. Your Honor, I'd now like to enter into evidence as a Defense Exhibit a printout from an online forum called Philly Beat. Specifically, a message posted by Detective Avalos on the forum."

"Objection," Donovan said. "Mr. Nolan hasn't authenticated this so-called forum post."

"I'm doing that now," Hal said smoothly. "Unless, Detective Avalos, you'd prefer to deny that you posted this message? Please remember, you're under oath."

Avalos's jaw tightened. "I remember now. We were both candidates for the position."

Hal nodded, pacing slowly before the witness stand. Kristina felt a familiar flutter in her stomach—she'd forgotten how captivating Hal could be when he was in his element.

"A position that only one of you could get," Hal said. "Correct?"

"Yes," Avalos said.

"A position that, after Detective Kirk's untimely death, you are now the lead candidate for."

"Objection!" Donovan's voice cracked through the air. "That's not even a question. Mr. Nolan is making arguments directly to the jury!"

"Sustained," Judge Booker said. "Save the arguments for your closing statement, Mr. Nolan."

"Oh, I will." He flashed a grin at the jury. "And it's gonna be a good one."

"Your Honor!"

"Detective Avalos," Hal pressed on, "where were you on the night of Detective Kirk's death?

The light caught the bead of sweat forming on Avalos's brow. In the jury box, a young woman in the front row leaned forward slightly.

"I was at home," Avalos said. A hint of defensiveness crept into his voice.

"Can anyone corroborate that?"

"No, I ... I live alone." The words seemed to catch in his throat, echoing in the now-silent courtroom.

Hal's eyebrows rose. "So, no alibi then?"

As Avalos squirmed, several of the jurors exchanged glances. Kristina realized her instincts had been wrong. Calling Avalos had been the right strategy, and Hal's questions were opening up cracks in the prosecution's case that would be hard to cover.

Hal shifted gears. "Detective Avalos, did you visit the police impound lot where Ms. Hess's Ford Explorer is being held? In case you need help recollecting—I believe you told me you did."

"Yes."

"You were in the courtroom when Desmond Cobb, an expert witness, testified that it was possible that a cop could have tampered with the SUV. Did you tamper with it?"

"Objection!" Donovan bellowed the word, but not quickly enough to stop Avalos from answering.

"You son of a bitch!"

"It's a yes or no question."

"No! The answer is no!"

"I guess we'll have to take your word for that, since you've been so forthright so far." Hal shrugged. "No further questions."

As Hal returned to his seat, his expression was one of cool confidence. But she knew him well enough to see the tension in his shoulders, the slight stiffness in his movements. *If this backfires, we've just thrown away Paige's best chance at freedom.* She found his hand under the table and squeezed it, feeling his fingers trembling slightly from the adrenaline.

"You did well," she whispered.

Hal gave a tight shake of his head. "It wasn't enough."

"Mr. Donovan?" Judge Booker prompted. "Any questions for the witness?"

Donovan looked shellshocked. When he finally stood up, Kristina's first thought was that she'd seen men on death row show more hope.

He approached the witness stand half-heartedly. "Detective Avalos, you've served with the Philadelphia Police Department for how many years?"

"Twenty years."

"And in that time, you've received numerous commendations, isn't that right?"

"I've received some, yes."

"You testified earlier that you were at home on the night of Detective Kirk's death, correct?"

"Yes."

"Detective, did you have anything to do with Landon Kirk's death?"

Avalos looked directly at the jury. "Absolutely not."

"Did you tamper with any evidence in connection with Landon Kirk's murder investigation?"

"Absolutely not."

"Thank you, Detective. No further questions."

As Donovan slumped back to his seat, Hal rose. "Redirect, Your Honor?"

Judge Booker's eyebrows lifted. "Briefly."

"Detective Avalos, you testified that you received 'some' commendations during your twenty years on the force?"

"That's right."

"And how many official reprimands for excessive force?"

Avalos's face darkened, a muscle twitching in his jaw as he stared at Hal. *Come on*, Kristina thought. *Show everyone exactly who you are.*

"You piece of shit."

A soft gasp from the jury box. A woman in the front row actually jerked back. *Perfect.*

"Objection!" Donovan shouted. The prosecutor looked desperate.

"Overruled."

"How many?" Hal said.

"I don't know." Avalos bit out the words. He looked like he wanted to lunge from the witness stand and pummel Hal.

"You lost count?" Hal looked at the jury with an incredulous expression. "How about a guesstimate? Are we talking ten reprimands? Twenty?"

"Objection!"

"Withdrawn. How many times have you been ordered to attend anger management training?"

"Objection!"

"Overruled. Detective, please answer the question."

"Anger management? Only once."

"Maybe you needed it more than once." Hal turned to the jury with a meaningful look. "Doesn't seem like it took."

"Objection!"

"Withdrawn. No further questions."

There was a sound at the back of the courtroom. Kristina turned, saw Aldo Burke leave the room in disgust. He let the doors close loudly behind him.

As Judge Booker called for a recess, she glanced at Hal, who sat down beside her with a tight smile on his face.

"*Now* it's enough," he whispered.

Kristina looked at the jurors. They had been shaken by what they'd just seen and heard. She could see it in their faces—the questions forming.

The doubt.

She leaned in close to Hal, her lips nearly brushing his ear. "Just so you know, I'm extremely hot for you right now."

Hal turned to her. "*Right* now?"

"Right now."

33

———

By the time they reached home, dusk had settled over the city. The adrenaline that had fueled Hal's courtroom showdown with Avalos had faded, replaced by exhaustion.

He stepped into their bedroom, loosening his tie as Kristina followed close behind. He turned to face her, feeling the corner of his mouth curl into a tired smile. "You know, back in the courtroom, you said—"

Before he could finish his sentence, Kristina's hands were on his chest, shoving him backward with surprising force.

"I know what I said."

The backs of his legs hit the bed frame and he found himself flat on his back on the mattress. He barely had time to react before Kristina was on top of him, settling onto his hips and leaning forward so her auburn curls cascaded around his face.

His breath caught in his throat. After all these years, the hungry look in her eyes still sent a jolt of electricity straight to his pelvis.

"Not that I'm complaining," Hal said, "but what's gotten into you?"

A wicked grin spread across her face as her fingers made

quick work of his tie, tossing it to the floor with a soft swish of silk before she started on his shirt buttons. "You were amazing today. Watching you in court ... I just...."

Hal tucked a stray curl behind her ear. "*You* were amazing. I couldn't have done it without you getting Booker to declare Avalos hostile."

"No more talking, Hal." She closed the distance between their lips.

His hands slid up her thighs, pushing her skirt higher. Her skin was silky under his fingertips. She looked at him and bit her lip in a way that made his pulse quicken.

He gripped her hips and rolled them over so he was on top of her. She gasped, her eyes darkening. He kissed her along her collarbone.

"Stop teasing." Her back arched. She wrapped her legs around his waist.

"If you insist."

Their hands fumbled at his waistband, urgent and clumsy in their hurry to undo his belt. Just as Kristina's fingers found his zipper, a crash echoed through the apartment. Hal froze, his legs still entwined with Kristina's, his heart pounding.

"What was that?" Kristina whispered, pulling back.

Before Hal could respond, the sound of heavy footsteps came from the other room. Hal's blood ran cold as he looked over his shoulder at the closed bedroom door. "Someone's inside the apartment."

Kristina slid off the bed and grabbed her phone from the nightstand.

"Bathroom," Hal whispered. "Lock yourself in and call for help."

"Come with me."

He shook his head, already positioning himself between her and the bedroom door.

Kristina hesitated.

"Go," he said. Another crash from the living room spurred her into action. She darted into the bathroom, the lock clicking just as their bedroom door burst open.

Three masked men stormed in. Hal might have recognized the leader by his build, but it was his cold eyes, visible through his ski mask, that cinched it—the eyes that had glared at him in the rearview mirror of the Camry.

And just like before, he held a gun.

The sight of the weapon sent Hal's heart jackhammering. For a moment, he was back in that courtroom years ago—his chest on fire, blood everywhere, certain as Kristina crouched over him that he was looking at her for the last time. With all of his effort, he forced away those memories now. Forced himself to face the intruders. He lifted his chin in a show of defiance.

"You should've listened to me, lawyer." The mask muffled the man's voice. Was it Avalos, or one of his goons? Judging by the anger, Hal thought it was the man himself.

"It's against my nature to lose." Hal tried to sound fearless—not an easy task with his shirt off and his pants hanging midthigh.

"Well, you're gonna lose now."

The cool air prickled his skin and his hand instinctively moved to cover the scar on the right side of his chest. The tissue was rough beneath his fingers. He backed up slowly, but there was nowhere to go. "We can talk it through—"

"You did enough talking today, Nolan."

So now we're using names.

"Is that so, Av—"

The masked man crossed the bedroom in a single stride. His pistol came up and whipped Hal across his cheek, sending him sprawling to the floor. Pain exploded through his face. He tasted blood.

"For once in your life, shut up."

The other two men spread out. Hal's eyes darted between them, his breath coming in short gasps. The silence from the bathroom was deafening. Was Kristina okay? Had she managed to call for help?

"Your partner in there?" the masked man said, following his gaze. "We'll get to her soon enough. On your knees."

"What?"

"Your knees, Nolan." He pressed the barrel of the gun to Hal's forehead.

Hal's body shook as he knelt, his heartbeat thundering in his ears. Was this it? Was he going to die in his own bedroom, while Kristina listened from the bathroom? *No.* The thought was too terrible to consider.

He was going to talk his way out of this, whatever this creep thought. *It's what I do.*

"I know it's you, Mateo." He forced a casual bravado past his split lip. "Why don't you be a man and show your face? Or are *you* the one who's shy?"

The eyes narrowed behind his mask. "You have no idea what you're talking about."

"How about your buddies here? Are they cops, too? I know you like to stick together. What do you guys call it—the Blue Line of Bullshit?"

The masked man laughed, a reaction so unexpected that it sent almost as many chills down Hal's spine as the sight of the gun. "You really are a piece of work, Nolan. Always thinking you're the smartest guy in the room."

"I'm *definitely* the smartest guy in this room."

"Can we end this prick already?" one of the accomplices said.

The eyes didn't stray from Hal—nor did the gun. "All you had to do was let the bitch go to prison. So simple. But you just couldn't help yourself. Had to show off, right? Be a big man in court? I almost admire you."

That's it, Hal thought. *Keep yapping, Avalos.* He risked another glance at the bathroom door, praying Kristina had managed to reach help.

"Whatever you do to me, it won't change what happened in court today," Hal said. "The truth is out there now. And you know what's going to happen after Paige is found not-guilty? That Internal Affairs cop, Everett, he's going to start looking at you. You're going down. It's only a matter of time."

In the distance, barely audible, came the faint wail of a siren.

"Maybe sooner than you thought," Hal added.

The siren's volume swelled. He heard a distant screech of tires. One of the accomplices ran to the window and parted the blinds with his fingers. "Shit! We gotta get out of here!"

"Time's up for you."

Hal leapt sideways just as the gun discharged. He felt the force of the bullet as it ripped through the air and embedded itself in the side of his bed. The room filled with the odor of gun smoke.

Kristina's cry came from the bathroom. Hal prayed she wouldn't come out.

The masked man tracked him with the gun, but before he could pull the trigger again, shouting voices filled the apartment. Men streamed into the bedroom.

The first man through the doorway was Mateo Avalos. "Police! Drop your weapons!"

Hal gaped at him.

The leader of the masked men spun toward the new threat. Hal slammed himself into the man's legs, jarring him just as his gun barked twice. The muzzle flashes lit up the room, but the bullets went wide, striking the wall.

"Stay down, Hal!" Avalos yelled as he returned fire.

Hal threw himself to the floor. A bullet whizzed overhead, so close he felt heat and the displacement of air. He crawled toward the bed, seeking any possible cover.

More cops poured into the room, shouting commands and threats. Gunfire erupted all around him and drowned out all other sound. Hal pressed himself flat, hands covering his head. A round struck the nightstand next to him, sending splinters of wood flying.

From the floor, Hal caught only glimpses of the firefight— Avalos taking cover behind the door frame, popping out to squeeze off careful shots, one of the masked men crumpling, the leader spraying bullets. Hal watched in horror as his shots punched a line of holes through the bathroom door.

Avalos dropped to one knee, his gun tracking upward, and fired three rapid shots. The leader's chest erupted in a spray of red. He staggered backward, his gun falling from his fingers as he collapsed to the ground.

In the sudden silence that followed, the only sounds were heavy breathing and the distant wail of more approaching sirens. Hal raised his head. His bedroom was a shattered, blood-stained disaster zone. The three masked intruders lay motionless on the floor, dark pools spreading beneath them. Avalos and the other cops looked intact, but shaken.

Avalos holstered his weapon and reached down, offering Hal a hand.

Hal slapped the detective's hand away. Shakily, he pushed himself to his feet. He'd made it halfway across the room when the bathroom door opened. Kristina was alive, pale but composed. Hal wrapped his arms around her.

"Thank God you're okay." He pressed his face into her hair. "I saw the bullets go through the bathroom door."

"I was in the tub. Are you hurt?" She studied his face, gently touching his cheek where the gun had struck him.

"Just a little pistol-whipping," he said, managing to lift his split-lip in a smile. "No biggie."

He let Kristina go and turned to see Avalos kneeling by the leader's body. Avalos got a handful of mask and pulled it off, revealing ... nothing. A stranger. A hard-looking man—Latino maybe?—with a scar running down one cheek. A face Hal had never seen in his life.

"What?" Hal couldn't help staring. "I don't get it. I don't know him."

Avalos leaned closer to the dead man, his expression grim. "I do. Luis Flores. Small-time pimp who thinks he's a big shot, runs prostitutes in North Philly." Avalos checked the man's pulse with his finger. "Dead now."

A pimp? Hal's mind reeled. "Okay, I admit ... I did *not* see this coming."

34

———

"Well, this feels a little too familiar." Hal tried to get comfortable in the hard chair of the police interrogation room. He offered Kristina a half-smile. "I guess being here as a victim is a step-up from being here as a suspect."

"The only way I want to be here is as a lawyer."

She sat rigidly in her chair, her usual poise fractured by the night's events. Hal hated to see her shaken like this—her hair in disarray, smudges of mascara beneath her eyes—and he silently vowed that someone was going to pay.

"I'm just relieved you're both okay," Lena said. She leaned against the wall, arms crossed. Since she'd arrived, her concerned gaze had not left them.

"*Both*?" Hal said. "Why, I do believe I've grown on my cousin-in-law."

"Don't push it, Hal." But the investigator seemed to smile in spite of herself.

The door opened and Detective Mateo Avalos entered the room. He exchanged an awkward nod with Lena before taking a seat across from Hal and Kristina. "How are you holding up?"

"Are the police done with our apartment yet?" Kristina said.

Avalos hesitated, as if choosing his words carefully. "Kristina, there are ... several dead bodies. Bullet casings. Blood. You should probably start calling local hotels."

Great, Hal thought. Another expense they couldn't cover. "We can sleep at the office for a few nights, I guess."

"The PPD has a small budget for residents displaced due to crime scene investigations," Avalos said. "I'll see if I can pull some strings."

"How chivalrous!" The laugh that escaped Hal's mouth sounded nasty even to him. "I don't know what your angle is, Avalos, but you can act as nice as you want. It won't change anything about the trial."

Avalos shook his head. "You're something else, Nolan. You actually thought it was me wearing that mask, didn't you?"

"I'm still not convinced you're not involved."

Avalos's face twisted. "Really?"

"Really." Hal stood up, despite Kristina's warning touch. He met Avalos's angry stare.

"And what happened tonight was what?" Avalos said. "An elaborate setup to gain your trust? Whether you believe it or not, I'm not dirty—and I sure as hell don't kill people over some courtroom drama."

The truth was Hal felt a strange mix of gratitude and resentment toward the detective. The man had saved his life—and more importantly, Kristina's—but he was still the enemy.

"Sit down, Hal," Kristina said softly. "Please."

Hal lowered himself into his chair, never moving his gaze from Avalos.

"We've got a dead pimp and two dead associates," the detective said. "Whatever you're holding back, it's time to talk."

"We're not holding anything back," Kristina said. "Not this time."

Avalos let out a derisive snort.

"It's true," Hal said. "Neither of us has ever seen or heard of Luis Flores before."

"You expect me to believe a word either of you says?" Avalos's skepticism was clear on his face. "Flores has been following you, violently threatening you, telling you to lose the Hess trial. Then he tries to kill you. Why?"

"We have no idea," Hal said.

"A home invasion on two high-profile lawyers is a hell of a risk for a small-time pimp from North Philly."

"And I'd love to know the answer, but I don't." Avalos sighed and Hal realized how tired he looked, how dark the circles were under his eyes. "That's the truth," he added. "I'm sorry."

"We haven't handled any cases involving prostitution recently," Kristina said. "And there's no connection I can think of between Paige Hess and this pimp."

Hal noticed Lena shift slightly at Kristina's words. The investigator's posture was always stiff, but there was an extra tension in her shoulders that hadn't been there a moment before. Hal caught her eye, and she returned his look with a tight shake of her head.

The conversation went in circles for another twenty minutes, with Avalos searching for any detail Hal or Kristina might have overlooked. Finally, he let out a sigh of defeat.

As they filed out of the interview room, Hal caught Avalos's eye. "Detective." He had to force the words out. Each one was painful to speak, and not because of the split lip. "I know you didn't need to answer Kristina's 911 call personally."

Avalos nodded. "Stay out of trouble so I don't have to do it again."

Hal followed Kristina and Lena out of the police station in silence, each of them lost in their own thoughts. It wasn't until they were inside the Camry that Lena spoke up.

"Avalos missed something."

Kristina nodded, pulling her seatbelt across her chest. "We're all missing something."

"No, I mean, he missed something *that we know*." Lena leaned forward from the back seat, a devious look on her face.

"And you didn't speak up in there," Hal said with pride. He pulled into traffic. "You're finally getting the hang of this PI thing."

"Very funny," Lena said.

"Are you going to make us guess?" Kristina said. "What did Avalos miss?"

"Delvecchio."

Hal gripped the steering wheel tighter as the memory came to him. "The angry parent. The one Kirk helped Paige handle, and then used to blackmail her."

"The one with scary connections in North Philly," Kristina said.

And Luis Flores was a North Philly pimp. Hal shook his head, fighting down a smile and the excitement coursing through him. "Kirk stopped Delvecchio from pressing charges against Paige—but how? Did he rough the guy up? Hurt him?"

"Maybe Delvecchio wanted a little payback," Lena said.

"Enter Luis Flores," Hal said. "Delvecchio pays Flores to kill Kirk and arrange things so Paige takes the fall. He gets revenge on both of them and barely gets his hands dirty."

"But when we started to dig into the case, Flores got nervous," Kristina said. "So he threatened us. Tried to make us throw the case."

"Can you find Delvecchio?" Hal said to Lena. "A phone number, an address?"

"Probably," Lena said. "But are you sure you want to talk to him? If we're right about this, he's dangerous."

"Dangerous?" Hal snorted. "He paid a pimp to do the messy work for him."

"This could be the final piece of evidence to set Paige free," Kristina said.

"And even better," Hal added, "a complete surprise for Slow Draw."

Lena leaned back in her seat. "I'll see what I can find."

35

"YOU SURE THIS IS THE PLACE?" Hal asked, glancing at Lena in the rearview mirror.

The investigator nodded, her eyes never leaving the house. "Positive. Anthony Delvecchio, 42, divorced, one daughter enrolled at Paige's school. He works as a mid-level manager at Philadelphia Federal Credit Union."

Hal stared at the modest split-level house across the street. "How does a mid-level manager at a credit union who lives in the suburbs get involved with a thug like Flores?"

"That's the question." Lena sighed. "He has no arrest record. Nothing I could find suggests he's anything but an upstanding citizen."

The early morning sun cast long shadows across the ragged lawn, lending the property a warped, elongated look. If their suspicions were correct, this was a murderer's house—or at least the house of a man who murdered by proxy.

It wouldn't be the first killer's lair he and Kristina entered.

Kristina shifted in the passenger seat, probably thinking similar thoughts. "Are you carrying, Lena?"

"Always. Anything smells wrong, get behind me."

Hal felt a tremor of nerves at the mention of her gun. "A dead body won't help Paige."

Lena shook her head. "If it comes down to us or him, he's gone, Hal. Do you have a problem with that?"

He met her gaze in the rearview mirror. "Last resort only."

Hal waited for her nod before he opened his door. The three of them approached the house together. Hal noticed motion in one of the front windows and had to suppress a shudder.

Hal paused at the front door, his knuckles hovering over the faded wood. He glanced at Kristina. "Isn't this when you accuse me of being reckless and taking too many risks?"

Kristina's lips twitched, the dimple making an appearance. "Do you want me to?"

"Well, you know." Hal forced a grin of his own. "Why break with tradition now?"

"You're a reckless fool who takes too many risks."

"You didn't have to call me a fool." Hal squared his shoulders and gave the door a hard knock. After a long moment, the door opened. The man standing before them looked nothing like the belligerent drunk Hal had imagined. He was skinny, almost gaunt, with nervous, fearful eyes that peered first at Hal, then at Kristina, and finally at Lena.

"Anthony Delvecchio?" Hal said.

"I knew you'd come eventually. Gotta tie up those loose ends, don't you? Didn't think it would be a woman pulling the trigger, but I guess that's fitting."

Hal turned and saw that Lena had drawn her gun. "Lena, what the hell—"

"Drop it." Lena's voice was flat, cold.

That was when Hal realized one of Delvecchio's hands was hidden on the other side of the doorway. It swung into view now, holding a semi-automatic.

"Hold on a second," Hal said. His heartbeat slammed in his

ears, his brain fixing dangerously on the two guns. "No one is here to pull any triggers. My name is—"

"I know who you are." Delvecchio aimed his gun past Hal, presumably lining Lena up in his sights. Only by some miracle did the Marine not blast him into oblivion. Or maybe she'd taken Hal's earlier warning to heart.

"Okay," Hal said. "So let's all put our weapons away and talk. I'm—"

"The famous Hal and Kristina Nolan," Delvecchio finished for him, "attorneys extraordinaire. And you brought along a hit woman, apparently."

"Lena is our investigator. She's just ... being cautious. That's all."

"What did you mean," Kristina said, "you knew we'd come?"

"To silence me. But don't think I'm going to die without taking a few of you with me."

"Don't be so sure," Lena said.

"Hold on. Just hold on." Hal moved his hands in the air, gesturing for Delvecchio and Lena to lower their guns. Neither did. "Why would we want to silence you? We don't want silence. We want a confession."

"A confession?" Delvecchio seemed to ponder the word, then barked a laugh. "You mean you want *me* to take the fall for Kirk's death? That's clever, I'll give you that. No wonder Hess hired you."

"Are you saying you didn't kill Kirk?" Hal said.

"You actually think I'd be standing here alive if I did?"

"You paid Luis Flores to do it," Kristina said. "In the eyes of the law, it's the same thing. Paying someone to commit a murder is the same as doing it yourself."

Hal's insides felt watery. His gaze locked onto Delvecchio's hand. He expected an exchange of gunfire at any moment. But instead, Delvecchio finally lowered the gun. He let out another bitter laugh. "I take back what I said. You're not clever. You're dupes!"

Lena surged forward the moment Delvecchio relaxed his arm. She disarmed him with brutal efficiency and tossed him headlong into his house. Hal and Kristina exchanged a glance before following her inside.

Lena forced Delvecchio into a dimly lit living room and dumped the man into an old armchair. Then she emptied his gun of bullets and placed the weapon far out of his reach, on a dusty mantel beside some framed photos.

Hal and Kristina took seats on a worn couch across from Delvecchio. Hal's fingers traced an oily residue on the armrest. He resisted the urge to wipe his hand on his pants. When was the last time Delvecchio had cleaned in here?

"Is this your daughter?" Lena said. She was studying the photos on the mantel.

"She's somewhere safe." Delvecchio's face became a snarl. "Somewhere they won't find her."

Hal felt himself rapidly losing his grip on this encounter. He leaned toward Delvecchio. "You believe your daughter is in danger?"

"Are you sure you're *the* Hal Nolan? The one who's supposed to be so smart?"

"We know you met with Paige to complain about your daughter's grades," Kristina said. "The meeting got heated. Paige pushed you. You threatened her. That's when Kirk got involved. Right?"

"Hess told you that? She said I complained about Josie's grades?" The idea seemed to simultaneously horrify and amuse the man.

"She said you were angry," Hal said. "That you went to her classroom after hours, confronted her. Are you saying she lied about that?"

"You did confront her," Lena said. The PI was still standing at the mantel, and now had one of the photographs of Josie in her hand. Her voice had softened. "But it wasn't about her grades, was it, Anthony?"

Hal's gaze jumped from Lena to Delvecchio. "I gotta admit, I'm not following any of this." He glanced at Kristina. "Are you?"

Kristina shook her head, her lips pressed in a tight frown.

Lena turned from the mantel to look at Delvecchio. Her eyes were actually misty. "When did you realize what was happening?"

The question seemed to bring relief to Delvecchio. He leaned back slightly in his chair and exhaled. "I don't know exactly." Hal still didn't understand, but he felt his stomach twist at the anguish in the man's voice. "It wasn't just one thing. Josie.... I'd find her dinner untouched. Hear her crying in the bathroom."

Lena nodded, encouraging him to continue. Delvecchio swallowed hard.

"Her clothes changed. Became more provocative. When I asked about it once, she said she borrowed the dress from a friend."

Kristina leaned in. "I'm sorry—what are we talking about here?"

But now that he'd started, Delvecchio didn't seem able to stop. "If her phone went off, she'd jump, scramble to answer it." A tear slid down his face.

Lena placed one of the framed photos in Hal's hand. It appeared to be a typical school portrait of a fifteen or sixteen year old girl, the kind taken annually at high schools throughout the country. But Kristina's sharp intake of breath made him look more closely. That's when he noticed a nasty discoloration on the girl's throat, almost concealed by makeup and a high collar. Traces of another mark on her arm.

"What the hell?" Still not quite understanding, Hal's gaze rose to meet Delvecchio's.

"Once, I saw her get into a car with a man ... had to be twice her age. She looked so small. I tried to stop her but—" He couldn't finish the sentence. "Then I found the phone. Not Josie's iPhone that her mother bought her last year. A different one, hidden in her room. There were texts. Arranging ... dates."

"Flores," Hal thought as a sense of dread threatened to overwhelm him. *The pimp.*

But Delvecchio responded to the name with a blank stare.

Then Lena said, "How did you connect the phone to Paige Hess?"

Delvecchio looked at her. "Most of the texts were anonymous, but there was one. Josie asked about an English paper due date. That's when I realized Hess was the other person ... the one arranging the dates."

Hal felt bile rise in his throat. Flores wasn't the girl's pimp.

His mind reeled. He'd seen dark cases before, but this was a new level of horror. He struggled to reconcile the Paige Hess he thought he knew with this monstrous revelation.

"Paige Hess was prostituting your daughter," Lena said. It wasn't a question.

Delvecchio nodded, his eyes haunted. "That's why I confronted her after school. I don't know what I thought I could accomplish. I was just so angry...."

Kristina said, "What really happened in that classroom?"

Delvecchio's eyes seemed to glaze over, lost in the memory. "Hess wasn't alone there. Two men were with her. Big guys—looked like ex-cons. Before I could even open my mouth, they had me pinned against the wall." Delvecchio's voice shook. "Hess ... she just laughed at me. Said she owned Josie now, owned all the girls."

"All the girls?" Hal's blood ran cold.

Delvecchio nodded miserably. "She bragged about it. Said Josie was just one of many. That she had half the girls in the school under her thumb."

For a fleeting moment, Hal wished he could unhear all of this, go back to a time when Paige was just another client. The simplicity of that ignorance beckoned powerfully. But there was no going back. He knew the truth now, and it was a weight he would have to bear for the rest of his life.

"How did she do it?" Lena asked gently. "Control them?"

"Blackmail," Delvecchio said. "Compromising photos, videos. She threatened to release them if the girls didn't do what she wanted. And of course, the more ... *work* they did, the more compromising material she had."

Hal swallowed. "How did Kirk get involved?"

"I threatened to go to the police. Hess told me if I made trouble, she'd make things worse for Josie. Said she had ... clients ... who liked it rough." He struggled to continue, his voice breaking. "That Josie would be assigned to them if I didn't back off. But I guess she thought that threat might not be enough because Kirk showed up at my house the next day. He made it clear no one would help us, including the police."

Kristina's hand found Hal's and squeezed it painfully. Hal barely felt it. Sickness swam in his guts.

The pieces were falling into place in Hal's mind, and the picture they formed was a nightmare. Kirk, the dirty cop, had not been blackmailing Paige about an innocuous argument with a parent. He'd been blackmailing her for running a child prostitution ring right out of her high school. And Paige had paid his demands, but only until she'd found a way to eliminate him. She was guilty—and not just of murder. Murder was the least of it.

"Where does Luis Flores figure in?" Hal said.

"Maybe he was just a rival pimp," Kristina said in the

faraway voice she used when thinking out loud. "Avalos said he was ambitious. With Paige in prison, he could expand into her territory, maybe even take over her operations. That's why he wanted us to lose the trial."

"But we didn't." Hal felt the blood drain from his face. "We're winning the trial." *Helping a child trafficker.* "Mr. Delvecchio—Anthony—you need to go to the police again. Landon Kirk is dead. He can't hurt you—"

"I can't take that risk," Delvecchio said. "Who knows how many members of the Philadelphia Police Department she's bought?" He shook his head. "I'm better off running. Hiding."

"Where is Josie now?" Lena said.

"I told you. Somewhere safe."

"Don't run," Lena said. "Just keep her there until this is over."

For the first time, Delvecchio's expression held a trace of hope. "Will it ever be over?"

"Yes." Hal met the man's stare, and his voice tightened with barely contained fury. "I promise you, we're going to end this."

"How are you going to do that?" Delvecchio said. "Aren't you her lawyers?"

36

Hal paced the length of their office, his jaw clenched so hard it ached. Kristina and Lena sat at the conference table. Their gazes seemed to alternate between concerned looks at him and expectant glances at the door.

The door opened, and Paige Hess walked in, followed closely by Ariana. Hal's gaze locked onto Paige, searching for any sign of the monster he now knew her to be. But all he saw was the same unassuming teacher who played the victim so convincingly.

"Hal?" Ariana said, a note of concern in her voice. "What's going on? Your message sounded urgent."

But Hal's focus was solely on Paige. "Sit down."

As the sisters took their seats, Hal noticed a flicker of unease pass between them. *Good. Let them squirm.*

"We had an interesting conversation today," Hal said, straining to keep his voice calm. He watched Paige's face carefully as he added, "with Anthony Delvecchio."

Something flickered behind her eyes, barely perceptible. "Oh? And what did he have to say?" Hal considered his poker face good, but it had nothing on Paige's.

He could feel his anger in the muscles of his jaw, his shoulders, his chest. "We know everything, Paige."

Ariana looked from Hal to her sister. "Hal, what are you talking about?"

"Yes, Hal," Paige said. Was there a mocking lilt in her voice now, or was he imagining it? He glanced at Kristina and saw the tense anger in her face, reflecting his own feelings. When his gaze returned to Paige, he thought he saw the hint of a smile on her lips. "What on earth are you talking about?"

"You've been running a child trafficking ring. You've been using your position as a teacher to groom and exploit vulnerable girls. And you murdered Landon Kirk when he tried to blackmail you."

"That's insane!" Ariana cried. "Hal, you know Paige would never—"

"Shut up, Ariana." Paige met Hal's stare, and in that moment, her mask slipped utterly. Hal glimpsed something inhuman, a void filled only with hatred and spite and cold malice, a depth of loathing that stopped his breath. "In high school, you never knew me. Not the real me. But now you do, Hal. The question is, what are you going to do about it?"

Hal felt his stomach turn. "I'm going to make sure you go to prison. And that you never get out."

"Are you?" A humorless laugh escaped Paige's lips, and she leaned back in her chair, revealing a relaxed confidence she'd never shown before. "I don't think so, Hal. You see, those crimes are all in the past—I couldn't risk continuing to run girls with the police watching me so closely, could I?" She tilted her head, pouting with mock concern. "But you look confused, Hal. Maybe your better half can explain why that's relevant to our situation here."

Hal's jaw clenched as he turned to Kristina. Her expression was grim. "The only time a lawyer can break the attorney-client privilege is to prevent a crime that has yet to be committed or is currently being committed." Kristina swallowed hard, meeting Hal's gaze. "Everything we know about Paige—everything Delvecchio told us—is related to her *past* crimes. We're ethically bound to keep her secrets."

"And to continue fighting for my freedom." A smile slithered across Paige's face. "Don't forget that."

"There's always a loophole," Hal said. "Some way out."

But the set of Kristina's mouth told him there wasn't one here.

"On the bright side," Paige said with a shrug, "The Nolan Law Firm will chalk up another brilliant win. And at the end of the day, isn't looking good what really matters to you, Hal?"

"I guess you don't know me any better than I thought I knew you."

Ariana, who had been watching the exchange with growing horror, finally found her voice. "Paige, this can't be true. There's no way you've been.... Oh God." She turned to Hal, her eyes pleading. "Hal, I swear, I had no idea. You have to believe me."

Hal wanted to believe her. The shock and revulsion on Ariana's face seemed genuine. But he'd been fooled one too many times since she'd first walked through the door of his office. "Get out," he said, his voice sounding low and dangerous even to himself. "Both of you. Get the hell out of my office."

"But Hal—" Ariana began.

"*Now!*"

Ariana flinched. Paige, on the other hand, remained unnervingly calm. She rose from her chair with fluid grace. "Come on, Ariana, Hal just needs some time to cool off." Ariana cast a final tear-streaked look back at Hal before Paige guided her out of the office. As the door closed behind them, Hal collapsed into a chair.

He pulled out his phone.

"What are you doing?" Kristina said.

"Calling Avalos. I'm going to tell him everything."

"Hal." The hard edge in Kristina's tone made him pause. "Did you not hear a word I said?"

"Screw the attorney-client privilege. We're going to make sure that bitch rots in prison where she belongs."

Kristina's eyes flicked to Lena, then back to Hal. "Lena, could you give us a few minutes? I need to talk some sense into my law partner."

"I guess I have some errands I could run."

Kristina held her silence until she and Hal were alone, then placed her hand over Hal's, gently prying his phone from his grasp. "I've let you bend a lot of rules, Hal, but I can't let you break this one."

"We've been defending a monster."

"She's hardly the first."

Hal stared at her, incredulous. "Are you seriously suggesting we continue to defend her? After everything we've learned?"

"I'm not *suggesting* anything. Whether we like it or not, Paige is our client. We have legal and ethical obligations. We took an oath."

"An oath?" Hal scoffed. "What about justice? What about innocent girls—*children*—being exploited and abused?"

"I love you, Hal. But taking the moral high ground? That's just not you."

Her words hit him like a slap. "Is that really how you see me? Some shady lawyer without morals?"

"No, I see you as a great lawyer who will fight relentlessly for his client. This case just feels more personal for you, more like a betrayal, because you knew Paige."

"I *thought* I knew her."

"But it's not personal, Hal. Not any more than the other trials, the other killers and drug dealers and pimps we've represented. It's business." Kristina's voice softened, but only slightly. "We knew going in that being defense attorneys wouldn't always be easy or fun—that we would have to defend some truly horrible people. And we have, many times. But if we change now—if we reveal Paige's confidential information—we could be disbarred. Everything we've worked for, The Nolan Law Firm, gone in an instant."

Hal sagged in his chair, suddenly feeling older than his years.

"I'm sorry, Hal. I don't like it either. But we're criminal defense attorneys. Defending bad people is literally what we do."

Hal shook his head. "I need to get some fresh air."

37

———————

AFTER A SEEMINGLY AIMLESS DRIVE, Hal found himself at the indoor gun range where he'd met with Avalos and Donovan at the beginning of this nightmare. As before, the smell of gunpowder hung acrid in the air, and each pop of gunfire threatened to pierce his composure. His instinct was to turn and leave. But he forced himself not to do that. To stand still for a moment. To breathe.

What the hell am I doing here? He wished he knew the answer. After his argument with Kristina, he'd gotten into the Camry and driven on autopilot, some part of him feeling a need to —*what, hold a gun?* It seemed ridiculous and yet....

Hal's hands trembled as he approached the counter. The same attendant was on duty. Her eyes flickered with recognition, but mercifully, she said nothing.

"Standard nine-millimeter, please," he managed, hating the quaver in his voice.

The woman pushed the clipboard with a waiver across the counter. Hal's signature was a shaky scrawl, nothing like his usual flourish. Moments later, he found himself in a booth.

The gun was a cold weight in his hands. He raised the weapon in a two-handed grip, lining up the sights to focus on the paper target at the far end of the lane. The silhouette refused to come into focus. Hal blinked several times before he realized what the problem was. Tears in his eyes.

"Come on, Hal," he muttered to himself. "Get it together."

The first shot went wide and the recoil jarred his arm painfully. The loud report made him flinch and brought him straight back to the courtroom, to Hazenberg snatching the deputy's gun, to Kristina's scream, to the searing pain in his chest.

"Get. It. *Together*."

He gritted his teeth, forcing himself back to the present. He adjusted his stance, remembering long-ago lessons.

The second shot was closer, clipping the edge of the target.

Then something inside him released. He emptied the clip, feeling a mix of emotions as he punctured the target again and again and again.

"Hal?" A voice cut through the noise, startling him. "Hal!"

He pulled off his ear protection and lowered the gun, turning to face Lena Randall. There was concern in her eyes, and maybe a little bit of pity as well. He didn't like seeing either. He forced a smile.

"How'd you find me here?"

"I'm a PI, remember?"

"You followed me."

"I followed you." She shrugged. "The real question is—why did you come here?"

Hal set the gun down, running a hand through his hair. That question again. "Honestly, Lena, I'm not sure." The words caught in his throat. "It just felt right, I guess? Maybe I needed to prove something to myself. That I'm not gun-shy. That I can still stand my ground."

Lena looked past him at the target. "Well, you proved 'gun-shy' isn't the problem. 'Gun-accuracy,' on the other hand...."

Hal let out a shaky laugh. "That bad, huh?"

"If this is your idea of 'standing your ground,' you might want to invest in a really good pair of running shoes." Her smile softened, and for a moment her resemblance to Kristina was uncanny. "Are you feeling better?"

"I don't know. This whole situation with Paige.... I thought I could handle any case, any client. But this ... how did I let us get pulled into this nightmare?"

"Paige fooled all of us."

"No." Hal shook his head. "We fooled ourselves. We took one look at her—mousy, quiet, meek—and we assumed she was harmless. Even when her story didn't really make sense. Even when we outright caught her lying, multiple times."

"But eventually we figured her out, didn't we?"

Hal let out a pained breath. "And now what? We just keep fighting for her freedom when we know what she's done?"

"Is that the real reason you came here, Hal? Were you hoping to find Donovan or Avalos?"

"No, I—" Hal stopped. *Was she right?* "Maybe on a subconscious level, I guess it's possible."

"And if one or both of them had been here, what would you have done? Betrayed your client?"

Hal opened his mouth. Closed it. Would he really have done that? How close had he come?

Lena sighed. "Look Hal, I'm no lawyer, but I know one thing. If Kristina says the law requires you to keep fighting for Paige's freedom, then that's what the law requires."

"What kind of justice is that?"

Lena was quiet for a moment as she seemed to genuinely consider his question. "It's the kind of justice our system is built on. Everyone deserves a fair trial. Everyone has the right to an attorney."

Hal scoffed. "Even when the attorney would rather see the client rot in Hell?"

"Especially then," Lena said. "That's when it matters most, right? When it's hardest to uphold those principles."

"Wow, Lena. You are *definitely* Kristina's cousin." Hal turned back to the shooting range and looked at the evidence of his terrible marksmanship. "So what do I do?"

"You're asking me?" Lena blushed a little. She moved to stand beside him, her shoulder brushing his.

"I guess I am," he said.

"Do what you were born to do—what you and Kristina do better than anyone else. Get in that courtroom and kick the DA's ass."

Hal laughed, taken aback by her words. "And if that means Paige goes free?"

"*If?*" Now Lena laughed. "She *will* go free. Because you don't lose."

Hal shook his head. "How can you and Kristina be so calm about this? How are you not all torn up inside? I feel like I swallowed broken glass."

"Oh, I can't speak for Kristina, but I'm absolutely disgusted." Lena's voice rose. "More than disgusted. Revolted. Angry. Furious. The only thing keeping me from hunting Paige down myself and enacting some good old fashioned vigilante justice is knowing that *you're* representing her."

"What?" Hal was perplexed at first, but then he saw the mischievous twinkle in her eyes—so similar to Kristina's—and her meaning sank in.

He felt something shift inside him, his paralysis finally loosening its hold. "You think I can still take that bitch down. You think I can walk this ... this ethical minefield ... and find a way through."

Lena's mouth curved into a grin. "Well yeah. That is kind of your specialty."

38

———————

HAL WALKED down the courthouse hallway, he and Kristina flanking Paige on either side as they maneuvered past lawyers, witnesses, spectators, and courthouse regulars. Stares and murmurs seemed to follow them with every step.

"This is so much more fun with everything out in the open between us," Paige said with a sly grin. "Don't you think so, Hal?"

"It's a barrel of laughs," he said dryly.

"Almost like we're conspirators."

A muscle twitched in Kristina's cheek. "I'd keep my mouth shut if you want him to do a good job in there," she said.

"I have no doubt Hal will do whatever it takes to win."

Kristina shot Hal a look, clearly not as confident in his moral degeneracy as Paige. "I guess we'll see."

Hal felt his stomach tighten.

"Nolan. A word."

Hal stopped. Detective Avalos elbowed his way through the crowd, moving toward them. Hal sensed Kristina tense up at the sight of him.

"Now's not a great time," Hal said, glancing at his watch. "We're due in court—"

Avalos stepped closer. "Give me ten minutes. Conference room."

Hal caught Kristina's frown from the corner of his eye. She knew how tempted he was to spill everything to Avalos, to unburden himself of the weight of Paige's awful secrets—and judging by the look in her eyes, she didn't trust him to be alone with Avalos for even a minute.

"It's okay," Hal said. He met Kristina's gaze. "Take Paige inside. You can trust me."

Kristina hesitated another moment, then gave Hal one final look of warning before guiding Paige to the courtroom doors.

Hal followed Avalos into a nearby attorney-client conference room. The detective shut the door behind them, enclosing them in the small space.

"You need to level with me, Nolan."

"I don't know what you're talking about."

"The ME found forensic evidence linking Luis Flores to Diego Messina's death."

So Flores had killed Messina, maybe as part of his effort to make sure Paige went to prison and stayed there, or maybe just a play for more territory. Hal kept his face neutral. "That's ... interesting."

"Isn't it? You want to tell me why a small-time pimp like Flores would kill a major organized crime figure like Messina?"

"You're the detective. I'm just a lawyer."

"For God's sake, Nolan, enough with the bullshit." Avalos's voice was low and intense—and, to Hal's surprise, tinged with desperation. "If I could solve this, I wouldn't be talking to you. I know you're holding back information." He leaned in, his eyes boring into Hal's. "I saved your life, Hal. I'm just asking for a hint. A nudge in the right direction. *Please.*"

Hal met Avalos's gaze. It took every ounce of willpower not to tell him everything he knew. "I wish I could help you. That's the truth, Mateo. It really is. But I can't."

"Why?"

They stared at each other for a long moment.

"I need to go," Hal said. He adjusted his tie. "Closing arguments."

Without waiting for a response, Hal exited the conference room. As he walked toward the courtroom, he could feel Avalos following him. And with every step, he had to fight the urge to turn around.

Judge Booker had already called the court to order. Hal felt the judge's disapproving stare as he hurried to the defense table and took a seat beside Kristina and Paige.

"What did he want?" Kristina whispered.

"Information."

"And?"

He shot her a look. "I'm here to win, not help the other side."

The courtroom quieted as Donovan stood to deliver his closing argument. Hal's hands instinctively reached for a pen and paper, props he always used during the prosecution's closing. Sometimes he took notes. More often he simply pretended to.

Donovan took a moment to scan the faces of the jurors. Hal studied their expressions, too, searching for any hint of the direction they were leaning.

"It's been a long trial," Donovan began. He adjusted the knot of his tie—which didn't need adjusting—and touched his impeccable hair. "Over the course of the trial, the Commonwealth has presented you with a veritable mountain of evidence pointing to one inescapable conclusion. Paige Hess is guilty. Let's review the facts."

Hal watched Donovan pace before the jury.

"Fact: Detective Landon Kirk was killed when a vehicle struck him. As Assistant Medical Examiner Julia Reyes testified, Detective Kirk suffered multiple traumatic injuries consistent with a high-speed vehicular impact—injuries consistent with being struck by a mid-size SUV such as Paige Hess's Ford Explorer."

Hal barely listened as Donovan described Kirk's injuries in gruesome detail. If Hal had ever felt sympathy for Landon Kirk, that sympathy had died when he'd learned that Kirk had helped Paige cover up her crimes in exchange for money. Fractured legs, crushed pelvis, shattered ribs, and massive blood loss leading to death? As far as Hal was concerned, Kirk had gotten off easy.

Donovan continued, his voice growing more confident. "Fact: Paige Hess's Ford Explorer was damaged in a manner consistent with striking a pedestrian. You heard this from our accident reconstructionist, Edward Huffman, who testified that the pattern of damage indicated a collision with a human being."

Several of the jurors looked doubtful, likely remembering Desmond Cobb's testimony contradicting Huffman's conclusions. If any had forgotten, Hal would be reminding them soon enough.

"Fact: Paige Hess was in the area, in her damaged Ford Explorer, at the time of the incident. We know this because of a traffic stop conducted by Officer Barrett Moody."

Donovan took a deep breath. "Fact: This was no random collision, no accident. As you heard from the victim's widow, Melanie Kirk, Paige Hess and Landon Kirk knew each other."

Hal risked a glance at Paige, and immediately wished he hadn't. She met his gaze, and her eyes seeming to gleam with the pleasure of their shared secret. Hal looked away.

"Fact: Paige Hess had a motive for wanting Landon Kirk dead. As Internal Affairs Detective Dean Everett testified, Landon Kirk was corrupt. And Paige Hess was making regular payments to Landon Kirk. His death freed her from whatever grip Kirk had over her."

Donovan leaned over the jury box for his final appeal. "Ladies and gentlemen of the jury, these are not difficult dots to connect. Paige Hess may pretend to be an upstanding citizen—a teacher no less—but don't be fooled. She's a murderer. All I ask of you today is that you fulfill your duty and return the only verdict supported by the evidence. Guilty on all counts. Thank you."

Donovan returned to his seat, and Hal had to admit the man had done well. He could see that many of the jurors looked convinced, others likely to be during deliberations. Slow Draw stood an excellent chance of winning this trial if Hal flubbed his closing.

But as much as he'd love to, Hal couldn't do that.

"Time for that Nolan magic," Paige whispered. Hal met her stare, but did not respond.

He rose, his stomach tightening. He straightened his tie, took a deep breath, and stepped toward the jury. He knew every eye in the courtroom was following his movements. Instead of making him feel like a star, the thought nauseated him.

A closing argument was always a performance. With Hal's head full of everything he now knew about Paige Hess, this one needed to be Oscar-worthy.

He pasted on a smile and began.

"*Fact. Fact. Fact.* Ladies and gentlemen, I think we've discovered Mr. Donovan's favorite word."

The joke got a laugh, and although Hal felt anything but mirth on the inside, he smiled along with the jury. The moment of levity did its job, puncturing the tension Donovan had worked so hard to build. The jurors leaned toward him, curious. Receptive.

"I like facts, too," he continued in a more serious tone. "But here's the thing about facts—they don't tell you the whole story unless you look at *all* of them. And Mr. Donovan isn't doing that. He's selecting. Cherry-picking. Why? Because he needs you to believe that there is no reasonable doubt as to Paige Hess's guilt —and the more facts you consider, the more doubt you'll have."

Hal could almost feel Wyatt Donovan's eyes boring into his back, but a prosecutor's angry stare was nothing new to him. He mentally shut out Donovan and focused on the jury.

"Let's start with the Ford Explorer. Yes, it was in the area. Yes, it was damaged. But as our expert, Desmond Cobb, testified, that damage could have been caused by almost anything. It's impossible to state with certainty what caused the damage."

He noticed a few nods in the jury box.

"Yes, Ms. Hess was in the area that night. Are we saying proximity equals guilt? If it hadn't been for a random traffic stop, no one would even know Paige Hess had been on the road that night." Hal injected a note of incredulity into his voice and added, "And while we're on the subject of the traffic stop, I'll remind you of Officer Moody's own testimony that Ms. Hess's blood alcohol level was 0.06%—below the legal limit—and that he let her go because she had done nothing wrong."

Hal turned, gesturing toward Paige. "Look at Paige Hess. I mean, look at her." Hal could barely do so himself—his very soul sickened at the sight of her face—but he hoped his audience would be too focused on her to notice his slightly averted gaze. "The prosecution would have you believe that this teacher, this woman with absolutely no criminal record, was somehow involved with a corrupt cop? Somehow became a cold-blooded murderer overnight? Does that really align with common sense?"

He moved closer to the jury box and dropped his voice to a conspiratorial whisper. "Now let's talk about those facts Mr. Donovan *doesn't* like."

Hal saw Donovan shift uncomfortably in his seat. In the gallery, Avalos looked equally uncomfortable. They both knew what was coming.

"How about the suspicious behavior of Detective Mateo Avalos, a man who admitted—but only after being declared hostile by the Court, mind you—that he stood to gain significantly from Detective Kirk's death. Rivals for the same lieutenant position within the Philadelphia Police Department. He also admitted that he had access to Ms. Hess's vehicle." Hal let the suggestion of evidence tampering hang in the air unspoken, confident that the jury would fill in the blanks.

"And what about Diego Messina? A known figure in the Philadelphia organized crime underworld, who just happened to be a regular at Foul Line, the bar in front of which Landon Kirk was killed. Coincidence?"

Hal sighed, as if a lifetime spent shielding innocents from the ravages of the state exhausted him. "You want a fact? Here's one. Mr. Donovan has worked tirelessly to distract you from other, plausible explanations for Landon Kirk's death. Ask yourselves who had more motive to kill Landon Kirk, whom we now know was a dirty cop—Diego Messina, an underworld kingpin? Mateo Avalos, a rival detective? Or Paige Hess, a high school English teacher driving home from her book club?"

Every one of the jurors was now leaning toward him, captivated.

"Ladies and gentlemen, I'm not asking you to declare Messina or Avalos guilty. All I'm asking is that you take a close, hard look at the evidence against my client, Paige Hess, and ask yourselves one question. Do you have any doubts—any reasonable doubts—that Paige Hess committed this murder? Because if you do, the law says you cannot find her guilty."

He spread his hands. "Paige Hess's fate is in your hands, but I'm not worried. I know you'll do the right thing."

As Hal returned to his seat, the courtroom remained silent. He did not bother to look at the jurors' faces. Their decision was out of his hands now. He did not look at Donovan or Avalos. And he sure as hell did not look at Paige. But he did glance at Kristina, if only fleetingly, as he settled in beside her.

She squeezed his hand under the table. It was a thank-you, an I'm-sorry, and an I-love-you squeeze, all expressed by a hand almost as familiar to him as his own. Hal squeezed back. Sometimes, no words were necessary.

39

———

"THEY'RE TALKING ABOUT US." Hal waved Kristina over to his desk. Three strides was all it took for her to cross their entire office. In their old suite, he would have had to call her. Despite the many negatives of this dump, he had to admit the close proximity was kind of nice.

Kristina perched on the edge of his desk. Her fingers absently traced the edge of her necklace as she leaned over to watch the broadcast on his monitor.

"Denise Moreno," Kristina said, arching an eyebrow as the NBC legal correspondent appeared on screen. "We made the networks."

Hal smiled, but didn't feel the usual thrill of the spotlight. Instead, a leaden weight settled in his stomach as Denise welcomed a panel of so-called experts to the broadcast, her plastic smile in full effect.

"We're joined now by Jim Freeman, former prosecutor turned defense attorney, and Dr. Renata Saunders, Professor of Criminal Law at the University of Pennsylvania Carey Law School. Jim, I'll start with you. What are your thoughts on Hal Nolan's closing argument?"

A distinguished-looking man filled the frame. "Well, Denise, Hal Nolan is known for his unconventional courtroom antics, and he did not disappoint. He risked losing the jury right off the bat—starting with a joke at a murder trial—but then he managed to weave together a narrative of police corruption and mob involvement that, in my opinion, completely disrupted the prosecution's case."

Kristina swung a leg against Hal's hip, giving him an affectionate tap.

"Could you elaborate on that, Jim?" Denise said.

"Certainly. Nolan introduced just enough doubt about these alternative suspects, Avalos and Messina. He didn't overplay his hand, didn't make any outlandish claims. He simply explained, in a way the jurors really can't ignore, that there is reasonable doubt about Paige Hess's guilt. It's a level of finesse we haven't seen from Hal Nolan in years."

The camera shifted to Dr. Saunders, a stern-looking woman who'd spent a lot of airtime dismissing Hal and Kristina as courtroom clowns. Hal held his breath, but the professor surprised him. "I have to agree with Jim here," she said, her voice carrying a grudging note. "I'm no fan of the Nolans' approach—and I think calling it 'unconventional' is too charitable—but I must concede that their performance at the Paige Hess trial was textbook. Hal and Kristina Nolan systematically dismantled the DA's case, piece by piece, and then built up their own alternative theories until those theories seemed equally plausible."

Denise nodded. "Dr. Saunders, you mentioned you're no fan of the Nolans' approach. You've been following the Nolans' career for some time now. How does this performance compare to their previous trial work?"

Dr. Saunders pursed her lips. "It's a return to form, in some ways. But also an evolution. A maturation. Frankly, many in the

Philadelphia legal community thought The Nolan Law Firm was finished after a rumored hacking incident brought down their practice."

"Ah yes," Denise said. "Jim—for our viewers who might not be aware, can you give us a quick recap on that?"

Jim nodded solemnly. "The Nolans have kept the details quiet, but apparently their law firm network was breached by cybercriminals who launched a ransomware attack that crippled the firm. They had to let go of most of their staff, downsize their office, even sell their personal vehicles from what I understand."

"And yet here they are," Denise said. "Dr. Saunders, is this a comeback?"

Dr. Saunders steepled her fingers. "The Nolans seem to have channeled the setback into fuel. Hal Nolan's cross-examination of Detective Avalos, for example, was a brutal demonstration of effective defense tactics."

"I'm glad you brought that up," Denise said, turning back to Jim. "That cross-examination was a pivotal moment in the trial. Can you break it down for us, Jim?"

Hal clicked his mouse, shutting off the feed. Kristina did not object.

He knew he should feel thrilled right now. He should be lifting Kristina off her feet and twirling her around the room in joyful abandon. Instead, he wanted to crawl under his desk.

"We're going to win this one," he said, his voice hollow.

Kristina looked as miserable as he felt. "It's looking that way."

40

———

The courtroom buzzed with anticipation as journalists, lawyers, and spectators vied for prime seats. Hal's gaze swept over the gallery, taking in the eager faces and tense postures. His eyes landed on Donovan at the prosecution table. The prosecutor's jaw was clenched, but as their gazes locked, Hal saw something unexpected.

He'd braced for a glare of righteous indignation, but instead found only a tired smirk. The realization hit Hal like a punch to the gut—sure, Donovan hoped to win, but he would also shrug off a loss without losing much sleep. Aldo Burke might yell at him—might even fire him—but even if that happened, Donovan would land on his feet. For Donovan, this trial was just another game.

The thought made Hal's stomach churn with a sudden, powerful surge of envy. When had this stopped being a game for him?

Paige, who'd seated herself between him and Kristina, leaned toward his ear. "Moment of truth, Hal."

Hal studied her, searching for any sign of the monster he knew her to be. It amazed him how well she played the frightened woman, fingers twisting in her lap, eyes filled with desperate hope.

"Keeping up the act until the bitter end, are you?"

"I've been keeping this act up since kindergarten."

There was a thrum of anger just beneath her flippant tone, and Hal wondered just how much her criminal exploits had been fueled by resentment, by rage at being ignored for most of her life.

"Do you do it for the money? Or because you enjoy seeing people suffer?"

"I've certainly enjoyed watching you."

The words stung, but Hal managed not to flinch. He held her gaze. "You want to know why I never noticed you in high school, Paige? Because you were boring. Ordinary. And guess what? You still are."

Her false face collapsed, her cheeks heating. Hal drank in the sight.

He leaned even closer to her. "You think you're some criminal mastermind? You exploit teenagers. You commit murder by running people over. You're even boring as a criminal."

She regained her calm just as quickly as she'd lost it. "It's killing you inside, defending me. You'd love to wriggle your way out. Well, sorry to disappoint you. You're on my side, and no amount of legal tap-dancing will change that."

"I haven't even started to dance."

The bailiff's voice cut through the courtroom. "All rise! The Honorable Judge Solomon Booker presiding."

Hal stood, straightening his tie as Judge Booker swept into the room in a billow of black robes. The judge's gaze widened as he took in the packed gallery. He grumbled something under his breath and settled into his seat.

"I see we're standing-room-only today," Booker said. "Let me say this once. I'm going to have the jury brought in, and this room will be silent. You will sit quietly. Respectfully. With decorum. The jurors have devoted weeks of their lives to serve at this trial, and I will not allow their hard work to be your sideshow. If I hear one squeak, I will close the courtroom."

He turned to the bailiff. "Bring them in."

The bailiff nodded and disappeared through a side door. A hush fell over the courtroom—at least for now, the mob had chosen to take Booker's threat seriously. Hal felt his heart rate quicken. He glanced at Paige, noting the tightness around her eyes. His gaze went past her and found Kristina.

The jurors filed in and took their seats in the jury box. They did a pretty good job of hiding their decision, but Hal saw too many glances at Paige—including more than a few from Ruth Baird—to doubt the outcome.

As the last juror took her seat, Judge Booker leaned forward. "I understand the jury has reached a verdict?"

The foreperson stood. "We have, Your Honor."

Booker nodded. "Bailiff, please collect the verdict form."

The bailiff crossed to the jury box, took the folded paper from the foreperson, and delivered it to Judge Booker.

"The verdict appears to be in order," Booker said. "Madam Foreperson, how do you find the defendant, Paige Hess, on the charge of murder in the first degree?"

The foreperson spoke loudly, even though the room was dead silent. "Not guilty."

The face of Josie Delvecchio flashed through Hal's mind, threatening to crack his composure. He swallowed hard, pushing down the bile that rose in his throat. By some miracle he held his neutral expression.

"On the charge of vehicular homicide and leaving the scene of a fatal accident?" Booker said.

"Not guilty."

And so it continued with each lesser included charge. *Not guilty on all counts.*

When it was over, Paige faced them, a free woman. "Well done, Hal. Kristina. It's been a pleasure working with both of you."

Hal opened his mouth to respond, but Paige was already turning away, her mask of innocence firmly in place as she faced the sea of cameras and microphones that suddenly filled the space between the defense table and the gallery as Judge Booker's demand for decorum was forgotten.

Hal and Kristina did not linger with her. They fought their way past reporters, past cameras and microphones, down the elevator and through the exit. The questions followed them outside, rapid-fire. Hal felt Kristina's hand tighten on his arm, heard her voice cut through the din.

"No comment at this time. We'll issue a statement later. Please, let us through."

Somehow, they made it to their car. Kristina slid behind the wheel. Hal slumped in the passenger seat. He leaned his head against the cool glass of the window, watching the city's buildings blur past.

Each office tower they passed seemed to mock him, reminders of a time when he'd seen this city as his for the taking.

"At least it's over," Kristina said.

"Like hell it is."

She looked at him, one eyebrow lifting. "I did hear you promise our client a dance."

"It would be a shame to disappoint her."

41

———

In a worn booth of the Chestnut Street Diner, Hal and Kristina sat across from each other, their laptops positioned back-to-back on the table between them. Hal struggled to focus on his laptop screen. His gaze kept darting to his silent phone beside the keyboard. Kristina's fingers flew over her keys, but she had her phone out too, next to her coffee mug. Their eyes met over the tops of their laptops, exchanging a loaded glance before returning to their work.

And mercifully, they had work. The Hess verdict hadn't exactly returned The Nolan Law Firm to its former glory, but it had made them the flavor of the week, and brought in a handful of new, paying clients.

"You know," Kristina said without looking up, "we can probably afford nicer office space now."

Hal snorted. "What, and miss out on the wonderful memories of being assaulted in the alleyway?"

Kristina's lips quirked into a smile. "I mean, if you really like slumming it...."

"I'll notify the landlord tomorrow."

They retreated into their respective documents, but Hal's

attention kept drifting. His eyes flicked to his phone for the hundredth time.

Kristina's voice cut through the silence. "Don't you think enough time has passed?" Hal looked up, meeting her gaze. "It's been almost an hour," she said.

The tension in her eyes mirrored his own nagging doubt—that their plan had failed.

He forced a casual shrug. "Give it a little more time."

Kristina looked like she might press the issue, but before she could speak, a shadow fell across their table. Hal looked up to see their waitress looming over them. She wore the look of someone who'd smiled one too many times that day and had no patience left for a couple of lawyers taking up valuable real estate and not ordering food.

"Anything else I can get you? Maybe some office supplies?" Her pen tapped impatiently against her order pad.

Hal exchanged a glance with Kristina. "I guess we could splurge a little," Hal said, his tone dry. "Pancakes?"

Kristina nodded, a mischievous glint in her eye. "Living dangerously."

The waitress rolled her eyes. "So, two orders of pancakes?"

Before Hal could confirm, both his and Kristina's phones vibrated. A jolt of adrenaline shot through him. He grabbed his phone, aware of Kristina doing the same. The waitress let out a huff.

Hal's screen lit up with a new message from Lena. A single emoji. *Thumbs-up.*

Hal smiled, the knot in his chest finally unravelling. "Actually, you can cancel those pancakes. We're all done."

———

LENA STOOD by the ancient coffee maker in the Nolans' office, trying to look busy while stealing glances across the room. Two men sat in a hastily arranged "waiting area"—mismatched chairs she'd pushed against a wall moments before they arrived—both unaware they were waiting for lawyers who would never arrive.

The men were Anthony Delvecchio and Charles Cooley, the Special Agent in Charge of the ongoing ransomware investigation.

Delvecchio's leg bounced with nervous energy. Cooley's impassive gaze caught hers. She gave him a pleasant smile.

"The Nolans should be here any minute. Can I get you some coffee while you wait?"

The FBI agent declined with a polite shake of his head, and Delvecchio didn't even seem to hear her. His eyes were fixed on the floor, his hands twisting together. Lena's heart ached for him. She couldn't imagine the hell he was going through—the hell Paige Hess was putting him through.

As she pretended to fuss with coffee filters, the silence stretched. Each man appeared lost in his own thoughts. Lena began to doubt the plan was going to work. *Not without some intervention.*

She walked over to Cooley. "Hal told me to thank you for making the time for this. He said he knows how hard the FBI works you."

Cooley regarded her with a curious expression. "It's fine, if he has information that can help with the investigation. That is why I'm here, isn't it?"

Delvecchio was looking at Cooley with renewed interest. As Lena retreated to the other side of the room, she heard him say, "You're an FBI agent?"

"Yes. Charles Cooley." He paused, then said, "You?"

"I'm a manager at the Philadelphia Federal Credit Union. Anthony Delvecchio."

Lena held her breath. After a moment's hesitation, the two men shook hands.

"I guess you're not a client then?" Delvecchio said.

The question elicited an awkward laugh from Cooley. "No."

"I'm not, either," Delvecchio said.

The mutual revelation that neither man was an accused criminal seemed to ease the tension between them. Cooley leaned back slightly in his chair. "What brings you here? If you're considering providing the firm with a loan, I hope you won't judge their creditworthiness from the office space. The Nolans are at the top of their game. They would be a sound investment."

"No, I'm not here for that. The Nolans ... they said they had some information for me."

"They said the same thing to me." Cooley glanced at his watch. "Strange that they would schedule two meetings for the same time."

"Maybe the meetings are related," Delvecchio said, his voice wavering with hope. "Did the Nolans ... did they mention me to you?"

"Not that I recall." Cooley leaned toward Delvecchio, his body language shifting as he seemed to study the man more closely. "Is there a reason they would have?"

Delvecchio hesitated. "The FBI is ... separate from the police, right?"

Cooley nodded, his eyes narrowing slightly. "We're a federal agency, focusing on crimes that cross state lines or involve national security. Local police handle more day-to-day crimes."

"Oh." Delvecchio's shoulders slumped. He lowered his voice. "So if the crime was a prostitution ring ... I guess the FBI wouldn't get involved."

Cooley leaned forward, his voice softening. "Not typically, no. Unless…." He paused, seeming to choose his words carefully. "Unless it involved minors or crossed state lines. Then it becomes sex trafficking, which is very much our concern." His eyes fixed on Delvecchio's face with an intensity Lena could see from across the room. "Anthony, I get the feeling we're not speaking hypothetically here."

Delvecchio swallowed hard. "Is there … is there somewhere we can talk privately? I think … God, I hope you can help me. And my daughter."

"I'm starting to think that's exactly why we're both here."

Lena allowed herself a tight smile as the two men headed for the door. Cooley paused at the threshold, turning to her. "Tell Hal and Kristina that something came up and we'll have to reschedule." His gaze met hers with a knowing look. "I'm sure they'll understand."

"I'm sure they will," Lena replied, her tone matching his.

As the door closed behind them, she tapped a quick message to Hal and Kristina on her phone—a simple *thumbs-up* emoji— and hit send. Mission accomplished.

42

—————

HAL RECLINED in his rickety office chair, feet propped on the desk, as the broadcast played in a window on his monitor.

"You're still watching that?" Kristina said.

"It's my new favorite show."

A news anchor on screen was saying, "If you're just joining us, we are live with a shocking turn of events. Paige Hess, recently acquitted of murder charges, has just been arrested by the FBI on suspicion of running a prostitution ring involving minors."

The image on the screen shifted to footage from an hour ago. Paige outside her apartment building, being manhandled by a pair of stone-faced FBI agents. She thrashed against the FBI agents' grips, her nails raking across one agent's face before the other could clamp handcuffs to her wrists.

"Feisty," Hal said.

Kristina shot him a look. "I think you might be enjoying this a little too much."

"You're not?"

"We're officers of the court, Hal. We're supposed to maintain a certain level of professional detachment."

"So ... no popcorn then?"

She rolled her eyes, but not before he caught her look of reluctant amusement.

On screen, Paige's eyes blazed with fury as she was shoved into the back of an unmarked car. Her voice, shrill with rage, was picked up by the reporters' mics. *I want my lawyers!*

Hal couldn't hold back the snort of laughter. "She actually thinks we'd come back for round two. Honestly, I don't know if I should be flattered or insulted."

Not for the first time that day, his phone vibrated, the screen indicating an incoming call from *Federal Bureau of Investigation Detention Facility, Philadelphia.* Hal made no move to answer.

Kristina eyed the vibrating phone. "You're not even going to pick up?"

"Nah. I think I'll let it go to voicemail. Again."

Hal turned back to the monitor, ready to savor more of Paige's public downfall, when a sound from behind him drew his attention.

A hesitant knock on the door preceded the entrance of a person Hal barely recognized. Ariana Hess stood in the office doorway. Gone was the confident strut, replaced by hunched shoulders and eyes that couldn't quite meet his.

"Hal," she said. Her voice lacked its usual self-assurance. "Kristina. I'm sorry for dropping in like this."

Hal felt his jaw clench, the muscles in his neck tighten. "Ariana."

"Hal, I was wondering if we could talk." Ariana shifted her weight from foot to foot, an awkward gesture so unlike her it made him blink. "Just for a few minutes. If that's okay."

"I don't think that would be—" Hal began, but Kristina cut him off with a gentle touch to his arm.

"You should talk to her, Hal. I was just about to meet our real estate agent about some office suites. I think you two could use some time."

Hal gave his wife a questioning look. She answered with a reassuring squeeze of his hand.

Ariana stepped aside as Kristina approached the door. She murmured a barely audible, "Thank you."

As the door closed behind Kristina, Hal felt a flicker of anger. "If you're here to beg us to ride to Paige's rescue again, you're wasting your time."

"I'm not." Ariana's hands came up in a gesture of surrender. "I'm here because...." Her voice faltered and a tear rolled down her cheek.

Hal sighed. "Alright. I'm listening."

"I'm sorry. I never meant to ... to bring all of this into your life. Paige...."

Hal felt his body tense. He wanted to lash out, but the pained look in her eyes caused his anger to soften. He guided Ariana to a chair, then pulled another one close and sat beside her. "I'm sure this isn't easy for you, either. Learning what your sister really is."

"I've been thinking about old times." Ariana took a deep breath, her gaze dropping to the floor. "You know. High school."

"Oh yeah?"

"Remember Cassie Gilmore's party, when I pushed you into the pool?"

Hal's mouth quirked in a half-smile, the memory bittersweet. "At least you had the decency to jump in after me."

"Oh, nothing we did that night was decent." She crossed her legs and her dress rode up, revealing an expanse of toned thigh. Hal looked away.

"So did you come here to apologize or to reminisce?"

"I don't know. Maybe both? Hal, my life hasn't been great

since high school." Her face moved closer to his, lips slightly parted. "I made some poor choices."

"I didn't." His words came out a little too sharply.

She regarded him for a moment—the sadness in her face achingly evident—and pulled back. She pushed her dress back into place, covering her leg. "Sorry. Had to give it one more shot." An awkward smile.

"Ariana...."

She let out a hollow laugh. "Hal Nolan, hopelessly devoted husband. Who could have predicted?"

"You'll find someone just as devoted to you."

"Maybe." She met his gaze with tear-filmed eyes and gave him a wistful smile. "You know, I still can't quite believe it's true. About Paige, I mean. All this time, I thought *I* was the femme fatale."

"Maybe it's time for a new role."

"What's going to happen to her, Hal?"

He shrugged, and his voice turned hard. "She's going to need a really good lawyer. It won't be me."

"So I guess ... this is goodbye?" She leaned forwarded suddenly and this time their lips met. But the kiss was brief and unexpectedly chaste, especially for Ariana Hess.

"Had to give it one more shot, huh?" Hal felt his mouth turn in a lop-sided grin.

A hint of her old spark flickered in her eyes. "Goodbye, Hal Nolan. Try not to miss me too much."

43

THE MORNING SUN streamed through the windows of Velvet Roast, a little coffee house on Rittenhouse Square. Hal savored the rich aroma of freshly ground coffee beans and house-made pastries as he settled into a chair across from Kristina. The bustling chatter of other patrons and the hiss of the espresso machine were a soothing backdrop.

No laptops on the table between them today—just two cappuccinos, foam adorned with delicate leaf designs. Next to Hal's cup was a blueberry muffin, its top glistening with sugar crystals. He took a bite, feeling content for the first time in months.

The sunlight caught Kristina's hair and made it shine like copper as she tilted forward. "So, counselor, what's your expert legal opinion on the critical case of Nolan v. Blueberry Muffin?"

Seeing her expectant look, Hal cleared his throat and adopted his most pompous courtroom voice. "Well, counselor, after careful consideration of the evidence before me, I must conclude that said muffin is guilty of being criminally delicious."

"Motion to compel sharing of said muffin."

"Motion granted."

Hal broke off a piece and handed it across the table. Kristina popped it into her mouth and chewed with exaggerated relish. He couldn't take his eyes off her.

"What?" Kristina said, noticing his gaze.

Hal shook his head, smiling. "Just thinking how lucky I am."

Kristina rolled her eyes, but Hal could see the pleased flush in her cheeks. "Flattery will get you everywhere, Mr. Nolan."

The coffee shop's bell jangled and Special Agent Charles Cooley ducked through the doorway, blue eyes sweeping the room with law enforcement alertness. Hal had to smile as the man approached their table. The agent's tall, broad-shouldered frame loomed over them.

"Hal, Kristina," Cooley said, nodding to each of them in turn. "Thank you for coming to meet me."

Hal stood and extended his hand. "Good to see you again, Charles." He dragged a third chair to their table so Cooley could sit.

"Do you want to order anything?" Kristina said. "The muffins are particularly excellent."

Cooley shook his head. "No, thank you. I won't take up too much of your time." An awkward silence fell over the table. Cooley cleared his throat. "I, uh ... suppose congratulations are in order. On your Hess case."

Hal watched Kristina tense. He forced a smile, trying to keep his tone light. "And I suppose congratulations are in order for you, as well. On *your* Hess case."

"Which we had nothing to do with," Kristina put in, "and was simply a fortuitous coincidence." She leaned forward and nabbed the rest of his muffin.

Another beat of silence. "Well," Cooley said, "I'm sure you're wondering why I asked to meet. Unlike our ... shall we say, aborted meeting at your office"—he paused, a hint of dry humor in his voice—"this meeting is to update you on the investigation into the ransomware attack on your firm."

Hal shot forward. "You've made progress?"

Cooley's expression was guarded. "We may have a lead. I can't go into details, but I thought you'd want to know. We're pursuing it aggressively."

"That's great news!" Hal exchanged a look with Kristina, then returned his attention to Cooley. "If we can recover the ransom—"

Cooley held up a hand. "I don't want to get your hopes up too high. Cybercrime investigations are complex, and leads don't always pan out. Also, a lot of times, the money isn't recoverable. But we're making headway."

Hal nodded, but there was no tamping down his surge of excitement. After months of FBI silence, he'd given up hope. Now, even this vague hint of progress felt like a win. "So what's the lead?"

"I'll have more details for you soon," Cooley said.

"Soon—as in not right now?" Hal said. "You're not even going to give us a hint?"

Cooley's lips twitched. "I'm an FBI agent. That's not really something we do."

"Seriously?"

Kristina reached across the table to place a calming hand on his arm. "Thank you, Agent Cooley," she said. "We really appreciate your efforts on this."

Cooley nodded and started to rise. "And I appreciate what you did. It won't be forgotten. Now, if you'll excuse me, I should be getting back to the office—"

"No, hold on," Hal said. "What's the point of meeting with us if you're not going to tell us anything? Someone tried to destroy our firm—*our life's work*. If you have a lead, I think we deserve to know."

Cooley seemed to study him for a moment, then apparently made a decision. He sat back down and met Hal's gaze. "The man who shot you, Oscar Hazenberg."

Kristina inhaled sharply. Hal felt the blood drain from his face. "He's dead," Hal said. "So unless there are hackers in Hell—"

"He had a sister," Cooley said. "Did you know that?" Hal's slack-jawed expression must have been answer enough, because Cooley continued. "Well, he did. A younger sister. Olivia Hazenberg. And here's where it gets interesting. Olivia served time for her role in a distributed denial-of-service attack against a Fortune 100 company. And she was released six months ago."

Hal looked to Kristina and saw that her face had gone pale. He licked his lips. "Are you saying that Haze—" He couldn't bring himself to speak the man's name. "That his *sister* is behind this?"

"No, I'm saying that our investigation is now focusing on a person of interest who may hold a grudge against you and who may have the expertise and connections necessary to have pulled off the cyberattack on your firm's network. But as I said, we do not have concrete evidence at this time."

Hal didn't hear the rest. Blood roared in his ears, the coffee shop's hum changing to static. Vaguely, he was aware of Kristina and Cooley rising from their chairs and saying goodbye to each other, of the FBI agent stepping outside into the bright morning sunlight, of the contents of his stomach—muffin included—churning and threatening to come back up.

Then his vision cleared and Kristina's face came into focus. "Hal, are you okay?" Her voice was soft but insistent. "Hal?"

"Hazenberg's sister." He smiled grimly as shock melted into anger. "Well, she's going to learn the hard way she messed with the wrong power couple."

"Is that what we are?"

"Damn right." He stood up, straightening his tie. "What do you say? Ready to remind Philly we're still its most infamous lawyers?"

"Why settle for infamous?" Kristina's eyes gleamed. "I'm thinking legendary."

THE END

Thank you for reading *The Legal Limit!*

If you enjoyed the book, please post a review on Amazon and let everyone know. Your opinion will directly influence the success of the book. It doesn't need to be an in-depth report—just a few sentences helps a lot. If you could take a few minutes to help spread the word, I would greatly appreciate it.

The next book in the Hal and Kristina Nolan Legal Thriller Series is called *Deal Breaker.* I hope you check it out.

—Larry A. Winters

Want to find out what happens next?
Pre-order the next book in the *Hal and Kristina Nolan Legal Thrillers* series, **Deal Breaker!**

Coming soon - pre-order today!

BOOKS BY LARRY A. WINTERS

ABOUT THE AUTHOR

Larry A. Winters's stories feature a rogue's gallery of brilliant lawyers, determined cops, and vicious bad guys of all sorts. When not writing, he can be found living a life of excitement. Not really, but he does know a good time when he sees one: reading a book by the fireplace on a cold evening, catching a rare movie night with his wife (when a friend or family member can be coerced into babysitting duty), smart TV dramas (and dumb TV comedies), vacations (those that involve reading on the beach, a lot of eating, and not a lot else), cardio (generally beginning upon his return from said vacations, and quickly tapering off), video games (even though he stinks at them), and stockpiling gadgets (with a particular weakness for tablets and ereaders).

www.larryawinters.com